The Invisible Red String

A love story that transcends time, place, and circumstance.

Peter Berlin & Ann Zachariah

Copyright © 2023 Ann Zachariah
All rights reserved.

Love knows no boundaries; it's written in the threads of destiny….

"An invisible red thread connects those who are destined to meet, regardless of time, place, or circumstance. The thread may stretch or tangle, but it will never break."

– Chinese Proverb

Table of Contents

Dedication
To our dads,

Mr. Jack Berlin

Dr. Zachariah Thomas

Thank you for your unwavering love, support, and guidance throughout our lives. This book is dedicated to you as a token of our gratitude for all you have done for us.

This book is a testament to the legacy of our dads, who continue to shape us, even in their absence. With all our love, appreciation, and admiration, this is for you.

Peter and Ann.

One

"An invisible red thread connects those who are destined to meet, regardless of time, place, or circumstance. The thread may stretch or tangle, but will never break."

— *Chinese Proverb*

As the first rays of sunlight gently kissed the horizon, a soft glow would illuminate John's cozy, 16th-floor apartment, revealing breathtaking views of the majestic New York City skyline. The towering buildings, adorned with intricate architectural details, seemed to stretch endlessly into the sky, creating a captivating tapestry of man-made marvels.

As John stood there, captivated by the panoramic beauty before him, he reflected on the remarkable journey that had brought him to this very moment. Each step he had taken and challenges he had overcome led him to this pinnacle of success. His advertising empire, built with unwavering dedication and countless sleepless nights, had flourished beyond his wildest dreams, casting a shimmering shadow over the city below.

John's achievements, like the breathtaking cityscape that stretched out before him, stood as a resolute testament to his indomitable spirit and unwavering determination.

John lived with his 8-year-old son, Noah. With a smile that could brighten the darkest of days, Noah possessed a superpower: Down syndrome. As a devoted father and a focused entrepreneur, John's world revolved around his son and his thriving company.

On a beautiful spring evening, John leisurely strolled through the inviting aisles of the local organic store. The air was filled with the sweet scent of freshly picked herbs and the faint whispers of laughter from the bustling farmers' market nearby.

As he carefully selected his groceries, John's eyes were drawn to a notice. It playfully beckoned him from its place behind the friendly cashier at the entrance, promising a hidden treasure within the humble store.

The vegetables here were nothing short of extraordinary, surpassing anything John had ever tasted. The flavors exploded on his palate, each bite a symphony of freshness and natural sweetness. But it wasn't just the taste that captivated him; it was the remarkable absence of the dreaded wax that plagued supermarket produce.

Here, the vegetables were pristine, untouched by artificial coatings, allowing their true essence to shine through. He picked up his groceries and hurried to the cashier. As he was swiping his card and making the payment, his eyes once again were drawn to the notice pinned to the board behind the cashier. He asked the cashier if he could take a snapshot of the notice. After capturing the image, he grabbed his groceries and hurried back home.

Noah entered the room, a burst of excitement evident on his face as he dashed towards his father. With a wide smile, he wrapped his arms tightly around his dad, squeezing with all his might. "I love you, Daddy!"

As Noah and his father embraced Martha, their nanny who had assumed the role of a loving mother to Noah, looked on with deep fondness. Despite being in her late 60s, Martha worked tirelessly as a housekeeper and nanny, not only to support herself but also to provide for her family back in Belize. Having come from a large family, Martha had taken on the financial responsibilities after her father's passing, inadvertently putting her own dreams on hold.

Noah's eyes sparkled with excitement as he animatedly shared stories about his friends from the special school over dinner. As

John gently tucked Noah into bed, a sense of contentment filled his heart, and he retreated to his own room. The steady cascade of water in the shower provided a moment of tranquility, but the notice he saw at the store popped up in John's mind, instantly igniting his curiosity. Donning a cozy, silky robe, he slipped under the covers, enveloped in a cocoon of comfort. In these serene moments, a subtle ache of longing tugged at John's heart, a yearning for someone special to share his life with. Yet, just as quickly as the thought arose, he dismissed it, surrendering to the embrace of sleep.

The next day, John rose from his bed later than usual. The sun was already high, casting a warm glow into his bedroom. He yawned and stretched, trying to shake off the lingering fatigue. Quickly, he dressed himself, opting for a comfortable yet presentable outfit. He snatched his work bag, ensuring he had everything he needed for the day ahead. Before leaving, John paused to take a moment to kiss Noah.

Standing amidst the bustling crowd at the local subway station, John found himself surrounded by a sea of people. Everyone seemed in a hurry, absorbed in their thoughts and agendas. John glanced at the digital clock, anxiously waiting for the train to arrive and whisk him away to work. As he stood there, a sudden craving for a second cup of coffee overcame him. The aroma of freshly brewed coffee wafted through the air, tempting his senses.

The temptation of the nearby coffee shop proved irresistible, drawing him in with its alluring aroma. Fueled by a sudden burst of spontaneity, he ventured towards it.

As he stepped inside, he was greeted by the familiar hum of conversation and the rich scent of roasted beans. He ordered a tall, aromatic cappuccino and found a cozy spot near the window. Sipping his coffee, he observed the trains gliding before his eyes.

In the reflection of the train's glass windows, John caught a glimpse of his own image - a tired yet determined man. He saw himself adorned in his success-emblazoned suit, seemingly mocking him with a haunting question: "John, are you genuinely happy? Do you harbor hidden wounds and voids? What are you waiting for? Join the group."

John, an introvert by nature, acknowledged the deep-seated demons and scars within him. He had always been aware of his emotional struggles but had recoiled from the notion of conventional psychotherapy. It required a daunting plunge into the unknown, facing his fears head-on. However, this opportunity that had come his way appeared far more benign. It offered a chance to attend the group, foster connections and friendships, and share stories with the promise of healing.

The group, led by the retired Dr. Kathleen Rodrigues, aimed to mend souls through the power of genuine human connections and shared narratives. Dr. Rodrigues penned in her notice that modern society lacked meaningful bonds, leaving individuals feeling isolated and disconnected. She was determined to revive that essence, initiating Saturday gatherings for a select group of five individuals at a time. The criteria for joining were strict: no significant mental health issues. Those who experience a sense of isolation or loneliness and an absence of meaningful connections in one's life are welcome.

Each participant would commit to attending seven consecutive Saturdays, devoting 1.5 hours of their time. The sessions promised a safe space for introspection and growth, a sanctuary where vulnerabilities could be shared without judgment. To ensure the utmost privacy within the group, all members were required to sign a HIPAA agreement emphasizing the importance of confidentiality and trust.

The idea of connecting with others, and finding solace in shared experiences resonated deep within him. This could be a chance to embark on a journey of self-discovery, confront his fears, and uncover new layers of understanding. With a newfound determination, he made up his mind. He would take that plunge into the unknown and join the group.

Two

"Important encounters are planned by the souls long before the bodies see each other."

-Paulo Coelho

John hopped into his black car, the engine purring beneath him as anticipation bubbled within. With a swift tap on the state-of-the-art GPS, he entered the address: Soul Haven, 1522 Village Street, Manhattan, New York.

As he embarked on the drive, a whirlwind of emotions coursed through John's mind, each mile bringing him closer to breaking free from the confines of his comfort zone. Excitement pulsed through his veins like a surge of electricity as he envisioned the transformative experiences that awaited him. Yet, lurking in the shadows were faint whispers of fears, reminders of the unknown that lay ahead.

Abruptly, he arrived at his destination, the sleek façade of Soul Haven beckoning him with its warmth and intimacy. The living room, bathed in soft sunlight streaming through a grand window, exuded a sense of tranquility. Green plants adorned every nook and corner, their vibrant green leaves lending an air of serenity to the space. Stepping inside, John was immediately welcomed by a group of friendly faces, their open arms extending a heartfelt embrace that erased any lingering doubts or reservations he may have had.

As Dr. Kathy led him into the room, an air of anticipation filled the space, momentarily disrupted by an awkward silence. The floor adorned with soft mats, bathed in the warm orange glow of Himalayan lamps, emitted an aura of positive energy. The room enveloped the soothing scent of lemongrass essential oil, which diffused gently in the air. With a welcoming gesture, Dr. Kathy beckoned John to take a seat.

With a friendly smile, she introduced herself. "Hey, I'm Dr. Kathleen Rodrigues, but you can all call me Dr. Kathy. You're all here for a reason. This is more than just a place; it's a sanctuary where strangers become lifelong friends. Soul Haven is dedicated to discovering harmony, restoring balance, and nurturing inner strength. Above all, we foster respect for one another, celebrating our differences. Consider this your sanctuary away from home, a place where you truly belong. But before we embark on this transformative journey, let's familiarize ourselves with a few ground rules".

First and foremost, respect. We hail from diverse backgrounds, so let's honor and appreciate each other's opinions and beliefs.

Second, confidentiality is paramount. What is shared within these walls remains strictly within our sanctuary unless expressly permitted otherwise. Here at Soul Haven, our focus is on healing, not romance. Therefore, during your stay, we kindly request that you refrain from pursuing romantic relationships with fellow participants. Once you complete the program and embark on your path, you are free to make your own choices. However, please remember that confidentiality remains of utmost importance. We are all here to support one another on our healing journeys.

Now, I invite each of you to introduce yourselves by sharing something you've never revealed before. It can be any aspect of your life. This will help us break the ice and foster a sense of openness and connection."

John confidently spoke up. "I run an advertising company, and I live with my adorable son, Noah, and Martha, who is like family to us."

Anna, the student counselor at the county school, introduced herself with a warm smile. "Hey everyone, I'm Anna. I'm passionate about helping students and proud to be part of this group."

Jake hesitated for a moment but then gathered the courage to speak. "Dr. Jake Abraham, but please call me Jake. I'm a cardiologist at Columbia University. It's a pleasure to be here with all of you."

Lilly, feeling a bit nervous, stood up and paused before speaking. "Guys, I think I may be the least qualified in this group," she said, bursting into laughter, her short brown curls dancing in the wind. "I tend to speak my mind without thinking. I'm a misfit in many ways, but I work as a nanny and truly enjoy it."

Dr. Kathy's voice echoed through the house, asking her husband, Mark, to join the gathering. With a gentle stride, he entered the room, welcoming everyone with a brief yet warm hello before retreating to his adjacent studio.

"How about we kick things off with some delicious, freshly baked cookies and a refreshing cup of detox tea?" Dr. Kathy suggested.

A tray of freshly baked cookies made its way around, tempting the senses, while Dr. Kathy distributed steel cups, each filled with her renowned detox tea.

"Oh, I fell in love with this tea in India!" Dr. Kathy said. "Let me tell you, it's got these four exquisite spices, like zesty ginger and tangy lemon halves, all mixed with invigorating tea leaves. Trust me, it's an extraordinary concoction. You've got to try it!"

"It's delicious," Lilly remarked, taking another sip to confirm the delightful taste.

"I think this one is good for digestion, you know?" Jake said, sounding convinced.

"You know what, this is what I grew up on!" exclaimed Anna with a big smile.

John quietly sipped his tea and just listened to what everyone had to say.

Dr. Kathy interrupted the tea-sipping session. "If I asked you all to describe yourself in just one word, what would it be?"

Lilly was the first to speak. "You know, like, a loser or something."

John seemed a bit off and replied with a flat affect. "Wounded."

"Punished for sins that aren't mine," Anna said, her voice choked with emotion.

"Broken but can be fixed," Jake said with conviction.

"So today, we're gonna start with a meditation session," Kathy continued. "Let's get into that relaxed state of mind. It's one of my favorite meditations. We're gonna do a grounding meditation that's super healing." She walked over to the music system, started playing some meditation music, and then sat on one of the mats with her eyes closed.

"Just follow my lead. You can't go wrong," she encouraged. "Let's start by taking slow, deep breaths in and exhaling. Inhale deeply, then release it slowly. Focus on the sensation of each breath and allow your mind to find peace. Now, bring your attention to the center of your forehead as you begin to relax your entire body. Imagine a cord extending from your root chakra, at the base of your spine, deep into the heart of the earth.

As you exhale, envision all your negative thoughts, self-doubt, hurtful words, painful memories, and past traumas effortlessly flowing through the cord and out of your body. Mother Earth will receive them, dissipating them forever from your conscious self. Don't force it; just let it all flow away."

The meditation continued for another 20 minutes, enveloping the room in tranquility. The only interruption to the serene ambiance was the gentle melody that continued to play, harmonizing with the soothing voice of Dr. Kathy.

"You can all open your eyes now," Dr Kathy finally announced. But nobody wanted to.

Anna was the first to break the silence. "It was an indescribable feeling of pure bliss!"

John gently brushed away the tears that welled up in his eyes.

"I have done this before, and with each attempt, it only gets better and better!" Jake exclaimed.

Lilly wore a profoundly sorrowful expression. "I had no desire to return. I experienced a serenity that had eluded me for quite some time."

"Good job, everyone! I look forward to seeing you all again next Saturday," Dr. Kathy concluded the session.

Three

'We are all broken, that's how the light gets in.'

-Ernest Hemingway

Anna arrived first the following Saturday, brimming with anticipation of joining the group. All her prior apprehensions melted away. As she walked into the familiar room, the soft scent of incense filled the air, and the gentle flicker of candlelight danced across the walls.

Anna rang the doorbell and waited. Soon, Dr. Kathy came and opened the door. "Hey there, Anna!" she greeted with a smile. "You're looking beautiful!"

Anna returned the smile, feeling instantly at ease in Dr. Kathy's presence. "Thank you, Dr. Kathy. I've been looking forward to today."

"Am I the first one here?" Anna asked, looking around the room. "I hope everyone else shows up, too!"

Dr. Kathy nodded. "You're the first to arrive, but don't worry, the others will join us soon. Please, come on in and make yourself comfortable. Help yourself to a drink. We've got the detox tea you all loved last time, and I also prepared some refreshing lemonade with crushed ginger and mint. Could you please get to the door if anyone else rings the bell?"

Anna nodded and walked to the table, pouring herself a glass of lemonade. Just as she took her first sip, the doorbell chimed. With anticipation, Anna turned to see John walking in. "Hey there, grab some lemonade. These are super sweet!"

John walked over and poured himself a glass before settling on his mat.

Anna wandered through the room, her gaze fixed on the lush greenery. Her flowing tresses danced in the gentle breeze while she donned an elegant, floor-length dress cinched at her slender waist with a delicate belt. Embroidery adorned the deep neckline, hinting at her allure and accentuating her graceful form.

John, sitting cross-legged on his mat, was captivated by Anna's graceful movements. A stirring sensation, long forgotten and buried deep within his heart, suddenly awakened, sending a rush of emotions coursing through his veins. Anna exuded an irresistible aura, a sensual energy that seemed to draw him closer with each passing moment. However, startled by his thoughts and the intensity of his feelings, John quickly averted his gaze, a silent reminder of the sacredness and tranquility of this healing space, where personal journeys of self-discovery and inner peace were meant to unfold.

Lilly entered the room donning a pair of ultra-short shorts and a casual T-shirt, revealing her slender arms adorned with an abstract tattoo. The tattoo depicted a powerful message: "I am a survivor," capturing both pain and resilience.

Shortly after, Jake hurriedly entered the room, his face beaming with a smile, straight from work in his scrubs. He quickly settled down on his mat and addressed the group. "Alright, my friends, what's on the agenda for today?"

Dr. Kathy kicked off the session with a captivating, guided meditation. Participants were transported to the sacred temple of healing, where the super-consciousness held the key to profound wisdom and transformative revelations. With the gentle melodies of the meditation music enveloping them, all four individuals embraced the challenge of quieting their conscious minds and attuning themselves to the boundless power of their higher selves.

As the meditation ended, Dr. Kathy turned to her small audience. "So, who's gonna share their story today?"

Anna raised her hand.

Dr. Kathy smiled warmly at her. "Ah, Anna, wonderful! Thank you for volunteering. Choose an incident or reflect on someone who deeply impacted your life. The one that rattled you to the core or taught you a crucial lesson. And, hey, before you dive in, no matter how tough the lesson, shower forgiveness and gratitude. Acknowledge the experience, be it good or bad. They were destined to cross paths with you, bound by some mysterious soul contract. You might not fathom it now, but trust me. It'll all fall into place eventually. Alright, let's kick it off.

Four

"And a woman who held a babe against her bosom said, Speak to us of Children.

And he said:

Your children are not your children.

They are the sons and daughters of Life's longing for itself.

They come through you but not from you,

And though they are with you, yet they belong not to you."

-Kahlil Gibran

Anna took a moment to compose herself, savoring a refreshing sip of lemonade. "Please don't judge."

Lilly offered a comforting smile. John and Jake responded with a playful blown kiss and an encouraging thumbs-up.

As Anna began her tale, a gentle smile graced her petite oval face while a distant gaze filled her eyes. Her voice, though soft, carried a certain strength and elegance.

"This is not my story," she said, "but a love story lost in the sands of time, swept away by the monsoon winds..."

Anna continued, back in the 1990s, I lived in a village called Chelad in Kerala. The roads, smoothly paved, meandered through a canopy of lush green coconut trees. Every day, the bus dropped me off at the entrance of our plantation home, signaling the start of my journey to college. As I walked along the narrow lane, wire fences kept mischievous cows at bay. On both sides, vast paddy fields stretched as far as the eye could see, accompanied by a stream with a charming wooden bridge. And as the sun bid farewell, I would sit on that slender wooden bridge and capture my fleeting thoughts with a half-bitten pencil on tattered pages. Scribbling verses became my refuge, and I transformed those very pages into little paper boats, and I watched them drift away in the stream. I never dared bring those words home, aware that my mother wouldn't approve.

"Listening to songs and writing such nonsense will corrupt you, my child," she would caution. "Dreaming, falling in love, or thinking about boys are against the teachings of the Bible. You must pray, attend church, and focus on your studies. In time, we'll find you a suitable match."

My old stone house had this grandfather clock that ruled the entire place. It would chime so loudly that you couldn't ignore it, marking the passing of time with each powerful strike. My mom, Mary, was the ultimate homemaker. Her whole world revolved around my dad, us kids, and our beloved animals. She'd wake up at the crack of dawn, around five a.m., and light candles before saying her heartfelt prayers in the cozy little prayer room tucked away in the corner. Then she'd head out to her vegetable garden, making sure she picked the freshest produce for our breakfast curries.

She'd whip up the dough for our morning chapatis with lightning-fast hands and get the water boiling for that rich black coffee

. As the aroma filled the air, she'd skillfully turn the dough into these thin, golden discs, frying them to perfection. She'd set the table with care and gently wake up my dad, Thomas.

I don't remember seeing my parents talk much or playing around. They never showed much affection either. My dad was more of a serious guy, always focused on running his local spice store. His mind was consumed by the ever-changing spice prices and how they could affect his booming business. He worried a lot, fearing that his enterprise would crumble and the impact it would have on providing for his family and marrying his daughters off.

My sister was like a mini version of my mother. She was all about tradition and discipline. She didn't talk much, always busy with exams and grades. I, on the other hand, was a dreamer, a bit of a misfit in our traditional, patriarchal Jacobite Syrian Christian family.

My parents were always racing against time. My mother often complained she had never truly known what it meant to relax. Meanwhile, my father's eyes were constantly fixed on the newspaper, scanning the latest prices of spices and tracing the rise and fall of the spice market. He was obsessed.

Beyond attending church on Sundays and making obligatory visits to relatives' homes, our lives were confined to the boundaries of our humble farm. I always dreamt of going on vacations, just like my friends did. However, my family never shared the same belief. My father would preach, "We must save every penny for an uncertain future. I am burdened with the responsibility of marrying two daughters. The cost of gold is skyrocketing, and then there's the matter of dowry." When he mentioned the dowry, the weight of the obligation seemed to crush him as if even the mere thought caused his shoulders to sag.

The farm's only festive occasion arrived with the harvest season. As the radiant sun bathed the fields in golden light, an atmosphere of celebration embraced us, infusing the air with excitement.

. The hardworking workers, with their sun-kissed skin and sweat glistening on their brows, gathered the ripe rice, carefully following a meticulous process to obtain the grains. Their hands moved swiftly, separating the grains from the husks, a rhythmic dance that echoed the beating of their hearts.

They worked tirelessly throughout the day. As the moon rose high in the sky, casting a gentle glow on the fields, we would come together to share our meals. Laughter and conversations flowed freely, and it was the time for celebration.

On the moonlit nights, as the stars sparkled overhead, the workers kept their spirits high. Their tired bodies found solace in the melodic tunes of folk songs that resonated through the night air. With voices harmonizing and feet tapping to the rhythm, they filled the night with music and joy. And we, captivated by the infectious energy, often joined in, creating a symphony of laughter, dance, and celebration under the vast, starry sky.

The farm, once a place of hard work and labor, transformed into a magical haven during the harvest season.

If you witnessed this, you would think that this was paradise. You know. They call Kerala, God's own county. Yet, a disheartening truth persisted. The laws of the land continued to govern every aspect of life, forbidding marriages between castes, religions, and social classes.

Love itself is deemed illicit, and only those vulnerable or morally weak dared defy societal norms by falling in love and marrying. Meanwhile, morally upright individuals, both young women and men, were subjected to meticulously planned arranged marriages orchestrated by the patriarchs within their families.

In the face of such challenges, the quest for true love becomes an act of rebellion, a defiance against the norms that confine and suppress.

My parents would proudly recount the tale of their arranged marriage. They would share how half of the village gathered to witness the union as two families came together, forming a larger and more influential kinship. They would go on and on about the grandeur of their wedding, done traditionally. However, despite this extraordinary celebration, I observed that their union lacked the depth and joy one would expect. Affection was a rarity.

Laughter and lighthearted banter were seldom heard. Compliments were never exchanged between them. Both were driven by duty, tirelessly working day after day.

On Sundays, we'd all get dressed up in our best clothes. I always wanted to wear a gorgeous crimson silk skirt with a fancy golden border, but my mom wouldn't approve. "Too provocative," she'd say, "and you don't want those boys giving you unwanted attention." I'd daydream about wearing bright red glass bangles and adorning my hair with fragrant jasmine garlands, but those were big no-nos in our household. Mom would remind us over and over, "We're Christians, and we have a reputation to uphold. We can't bring shame to our family name."

"Anna, Anna," my mom's voice grew impatient. I was sitting on a low branch of a mango tree, just watching those dark clouds gathering on the horizon. The sky was getting darker, and the wind was picking up speed. It was about to pour down with the fury of the monsoons. I loved the rain, you know? I would often walk in the rain without an umbrella, enjoying every moment, feeling so free as the raindrops soaked me. But there was Mom, standing at the base of the tree, her face all red with anger. "It's going to rain, don't you know?" she scolded. "Come inside the house. I've told you so many times I don't like girls climbing trees."

Walking into the room, she delicately brushed away the raindrops from my hair with her saree. As we gathered around the dinner table, my excitement was palpable. "Ma," I exclaimed, "I'm thrilled that college is reopening tomorrow! I can't wait to make new friends."

Ma offered me a gentle reminder. "Remember, there will be male students at college. Ignore them. Make friends only with girls. Don't bring any bad name to the family. People are watching you."

Little did anyone know what was about to unfold and how profoundly it would impact my life. At that moment, I was oblivious, perhaps by design.

Anna delicately lifted her glass, and sipped her coffee, while the eager group grew restless, urging her to continue the story. "Maybe I'll carry on next week," she suggested.

Dr. Kathy intervened, insisting, "No, Anna, please continue. You can't leave us in suspense like this!"

Anna put her glass down gently and continued with her story, "During that time, I was roughly 22 years old, pursuing my master's degree in psychology at college. I aspired to become a therapist, just like Dr. Kathy. Our college boasted expansive gardens and spacious corridors, housed within a charming red brick building spanning four stories. One month passed without any significant incidents.

Then, on that fateful day, I met him. He had bright eyes and a warm smile. I found myself looking at him. Maybe staring would be the right word. No, it wasn't love at first sight. It was a soul pull, a force that tugged at the very essence of my being. How does one possibly explain such a phenomenon?

On the day of the music festival, the college buzzed with excitement and joy. As I descended the stairs, he ascended towards me. Despite my attempts to avert my gaze, our eyes met directly. The moment was awkward. "Hey there, I'm Krishna," he said.

"Anna," I whispered.

He smiled, his eyes sparkling. "Would you like to join me for a cup of coffee?" he asked, his smile growing wider.

Despite my apprehension, a strong desire welled up within me to get to know him better, and so I found the courage to say, "Yes."

We got coffee and spent the evening talking about various things. We shared our dreams, aspirations, and hopes as we talked. I learned that he was a year ahead of me in college, studying Information Technology. He liked to explore new places and often went on hikes around the city. We shared so many similarities in terms of interests and academic background that I felt like I had known him for years, not the few hours we had spent together.

We quickly formed a close friendship and began spending a lot of time together. Whenever we met outside of college, it had to be done discreetly and in secret. I would go to the nearby farm with my girlfriend while he would cycle there. We would sit by the stream, engaging in deep conversations, while our friend Rekha would sit nearby, engrossed in one or two romance novels.

Once, I asked him to make a promise - that we would forever remain the best of friends and never cross the line and fall in love. Love, I believed, was off-limits, but friendship was permissible. As a Christian girl, I knew that marrying a Hindu boy was forbidden by law, and it was a boundary that should never be crossed. It was the law of the land. It was the law of the tradition, and it was followed for generations.

Our friendship provided comfort and acceptance. Krishna embraced it. He knew as much as I did that only a friendship was permitted between a Christian girl and a Hindu boy. That was needed for the survival of our tribe, or so they said.

In the depths of the woods, we had a special place we called our secret garden of butterflies. I used to share my poems with Krishna there, and he cherished every word. Before Krishna, my verses were steeped in spirituality and inspiration, but with him, they blossomed with hues of love. Though love remained unspoken, unconfessed, and undefined, we shared an inexplicable bond, a profound connection that only souls could feel and know.

One evening, Krishna was nowhere to be seen at our pre-planned time, and I grew restless with every passing second. Rekha's warning reverberated in my mind - if Krishna didn't show up soon, we would have to leave. Minutes slipped away, and impatience started to choke me., intensifying my yearning to see him.

Just as I was on the verge of surrendering to disappointment, he came from behind and hugged me. "Show me your hand, Anna." He had a surprise in store. I stretched out my hand, and he slipped these crimson-red glass bangles on my hand.

Soon, I mustered up enough courage to set Rekha free, and it was just the two of us in our enchanting butterfly garden. Sometimes, we would bask in the gentle rain, sitting there intertwined in perfect silence, and at times, I would lay on his lap and engage in childlike banter.

Krishna held a deep love for every living being, and it seemed that even the birds and butterflies were drawn to his magnetic presence. He would bring paper cups from his home and fill them with water for the thirsty birds to drink. Though love was forbidden, an unspoken yearning for deeper affection began to stir within me.

One day, I gathered the courage to ask him to kiss me like a friend. He burst into laughter, his voice carrying a hint of mischief. "How does one kiss like that?" he asked. I suggested a gentle kiss on my cheek. He pulled me close, embracing me tightly for what felt like an eternity, and on that day, I experienced my first kiss. With his hands cradling my face, he drew me nearer, teasing my lips with a tender brush until I allowed him to deepen the kiss, delving into the depths of our souls.

We both recognized at that moment that our connection was forged in the depths of our souls, tested by the fires of life. Parting ways would not be easy, perhaps even impossible. Religion loomed between us like an immovable steel wall. It was Krishna who broached the subject, proposing, "Can't we simply live our lives, believing in whatever we choose? You pray to your God, and I can pray to mine."

"And what about our children?" I asked.

His laughter grew even louder as he replied, "They will be the luckiest, for they shall have the watchful eyes of many Gods upon them."

"I pondered over the thought, considering it acceptable. However, I couldn't help but wonder about what lies beyond death. I asked, "If I were to pass away, the church would want me buried, while the temple would prefer cremation for you."

He stared at me as if I had lost my mind. "Anna, why are we thinking about death already? We haven't even begun our life".

We weaved our plans and penned our dreams in the ever-shifting currents of time. Once Krishna secures a job, we'll escape far away from the village and start a new chapter in a distant corner of the world, where love and freedom are ours to embrace.

This silent promise wove a cocoon of security around our relationship, nurturing our beautiful bond. As we ventured deeper into each other's worlds, the boundaries that once stood guard began to fade away like morning mist in the warmth of the sun. Under the watchful gaze of the majestic mango tree, beside the babbling stream that whispered secrets, in the heart of the enchanted woods, within our secret garden teeming with butterflies, Krishna and I shared a love that transcended the physical realm.

His touch ignited dormant senses within me, awakening a symphony of emotions that danced to the rhythm of our hearts. With every caress, I felt a profound sense of beauty, an untamed feminine energy that surged through my veins, infusing me with the audacity and fortitude to conquer any obstacle that dared cross our path.

Change is an inevitable truth, they say. But what if dreams are ephemeral mists at dawn, dissipating swiftly? Little did I anticipate that my dreams and love would soon collide with an untimely demise, leaving behind a poignant tale.

The crimson glass bangles and their delicate chime awakened a profound sense of love within me, but alas, it was these very bangles that eventually led to its death. When I returned home, I carefully concealed the bangles in the deepest drawers of my room, hiding them beneath layers of garments, ensuring their secrecy.

It was that Sunday morning when Mama seemed restless. She couldn't find her white saree to wear to church, so she searched through all the drawers. She even came into my tiny room and started rummaging through the clothes. Before I could say anything, she found a small brown paper packet with those glass bangles. Mama got mad and demanded to know where I got them and why I hid them.

I didn't even have time to devise an excuse when my sister burst into the room, wearing a big smile on her face. She loudly said, "Ma, Krishna gave them to Anna! You know, Krishna, the Hindu boy from her college. They meet in secret whenever she says she's going for tuition with Rekha. I've seen them together. One day, I even followed them."

By that point, my father had succumbed to the chaos. Mama raised her hand and delivered a stinging slap across my face. "It's so disgraceful," my father uttered with disappointment. They departed, slamming the door behind them. The house was engulfed in an eerie silence. No words were exchanged around the dinner table.

As I prepared for college the following day, my father entered my room, and with a serious look on his face, he said, "It's over. You will no longer pursue your education."

All the cries and pleas amounted to nothing. They were met with indifference, and I eventually yielded, resigning myself to my fate.

It had just been six months since my life took an unexpected turn. One Saturday evening, my mom was very kind to me and seemed so happy. "You're such a lucky girl, you know?" she said. "So many girls would kill for this opportunity. They couldn't even dream of it! Remember Dad's friend Sam, who lives in America? Well, he and his family are coming to India, and they want to meet you. They even want Alex to marry you. Can you believe it?"

I tried explaining my reservations to my mom, but she didn't want to hear it. "They've seen your picture, and Alex is interested in you," she insisted.

"But Ma," I protested, "he doesn't even know me."

"What's there to know?" she replied. "You have a whole lifetime to get to know each other."

Just then, Dad walked in and said that there would be no more discussions on the matter. It was settled.

During the "meet-the-bride" meeting, Alex and I did not engage in any conversations. He appeared half-asleep, with droopy eyelids. It was explained that he was experiencing jet lag due to the long and arduous flight.

Our wedding took place in June, and on that day, the monsoons raged like never before. The rain poured down in sheets, drenching the entire town. After all the rituals had been completed, we were ushered to our room, where I was expected to consummate my marriage. I lay there on the bed, tears streaming down my face as it truly dawned upon me that this was my future, my life now.

Alex entered the room and undressed, gesturing for me to do the same. He believed that the consummation of marriage should happen on the wedding night. After the mechanical sexual encounter, he inspected the bed sheets for any sign of blood. Not finding any, his shock silenced him as he struggled to ask, "Are you not a virgin?" Despite his fear and surprise, he did not attempt to resume the conversation and hastily retreated to the bathroom to clean up.

In the following months, I felt trapped in the world of Alex and his family. It was a world where traditional values held strong, and his parents expected nothing less than unwavering adherence to their rules. As the eldest son, Alex often found himself caught in the crosshairs of their constant interjections into our affairs. But the matriarch of the family truly held the reins, exercising control over every aspect of our lives.

As the days passed, I started to feel more like an outsider thrust into a family that I could not understand at family gatherings. I felt lonely and isolated. I occupied a space that felt simultaneously present and distant. My existence, or lack thereof, held little significance for anyone. I was a palpable yet invisible force of human energy.

The days followed a ritual: Alex remained mostly silent. In the mornings, I would wake up and prepare breakfast for Alex. He would then depart for work, barely uttering a word. Upon returning home, he would have his dinner before retiring for the night. He had a strong preference for order, almost an obsession with perfection. Any deviation from the inflexible patterns would trigger his explosive anger. Realizing this, I made every effort to ensure that everything aligned concretely, following the patterns or orders that he lived by.

From the way he showered to the seat he occupied at the dining table, everything had its designated place. Even his cutlery had to be arranged in a specific way when he ate. Bread required a separate plate, while curries were served in small steel bowls.

Even in bed, he adhered to a strict ritual. Sensuality and affection were foreign concepts to him. For Alex, a disciplined approach to sex was the norm. He couldn't quite explain why he engaged in such acts, but he believed it reflected his masculinity and duty as a husband. And for him, that was all that mattered.

My life revolved around cooking Alex's favorite dishes and cleaning the house. Even a single human hair found in the bathroom was enough to unleash his anger. "You don't have a job. You're sitting here doing nothing. And you can't even clean the bathroom properly?" he would yell.

As time passed, living within the confines of both the physical walls of our home and the emotional walls of my heart, I began to accept this as the norm. I didn't know anything different, and I forgot what normal was.

My dreams and emotions faded away. I ate very little. I hardly smiled. I felt like I was walking on eggshells all the time.

Interestingly, I had no grievances either. I existed between apathy and emotional numbness in a plane of primitive existence. I didn't have any friends. I wasn't allowed to have any. I couldn't confide in my parents about anything. They didn't want to listen. They were relieved that I didn't run away with a Hindu boy and got married instead and then moved to America. I tried to talk to my mother, but she said, "Every marriage has its challenges. You need to learn how to adapt. If your husband is always angry, kneel and pray to God. And if he lacks affection, it means you're not satisfying him sexually. You need to please him to earn his favor."

Day by day, Alex's anger intensified, trapping him in an unyielding state of rage. Meanwhile, I enrolled in school to pursue a master's degree in psychology. That decision turned out to be the best one I've made in a long while. Finally, I could breathe freely.

At first, it was a bit tough to open up and make friends. The girl I used to be, all thin with long hair and that mischievous grin, who fearlessly embraced love, felt like a distant memory. Like she was hidden and hibernating behind the person I had become. But the class was filled with incredible individuals who were so into exploring the depths of the human psyche. And among them, there was Lauren. When our paths crossed, she was already six months pregnant. She radiated happiness and had this remarkable openness about her. It was beautiful to witness how she embraced this new chapter in her life with such grace and joy. Her presence in the class added a unique and heartwarming dynamic, and it made me appreciate the diversity of experiences and journeys we all bring to the table.

Lauren would always come and find a place next to me in class. One day, she noticed I was wearing the same pair of jeans and two T-shirts. She approached me and said, "Hey Anna, I'm six months pregnant and can't fit into my old clothes anymore. If you don't mind, I'd be happy to give them all to you."

I was so grateful for her kindness and accepted her offer. She even drove me to her house. We sat down and enjoyed tea together, and I got to meet her husband, who was bubbling with excitement about their baby on the way.

When I returned home and opened the bag she gave me, I found beautiful dresses, a makeup kit, a pair of earrings, and a necklace. There was a little note from Lauren that read, "I hope you love these, Anna. I thought you would look stunning with some makeup and those earrings."

I adorned myself in Lauren's beautiful dress, carefully draping the luxurious fabric that gracefully hugged my figure. With a gentle touch, I allowed my wavy hair to cascade naturally down to my waist. I then wore the earrings and the necklace. With a steady hand, I applied the eyeliner, skillfully accentuating my eyes, and put on the pink lipstick.

As I gazed upon my reflection, I felt like the Anna I left behind.

When I graduated with distinction, Alex's distress deepened. It became apparent that his father held traditional views on marriage and expected him to exert control over me. "You should control your wife," his father would say often, echoing the sentiment of his mother, who believed that an ideal woman should be submissive to her husband. This clash of values created tension within our relationship.

However, despite the challenges we faced, I managed to secure a job as a school counselor, which brought a sense of stability with its regular paychecks. Alex was happy about that. I would hand him my paychecks, and he would give me $10 daily for my expenses. He would lay the $10 bill on the kitchen counter for me. Sometimes, I skipped lunch to save the extra, add it up, and buy some dress or make-up.

As time passed, the strain on our relationship grew. We began to drift apart, gradually becoming more distant and disconnected. The conflicting expectations placed upon us and the lack of shared goals took a toll on our connection, leading to a sense of dissonance between us. The verbal abuse persisted, occasionally escalating into physical abuse.

Honestly, I used to believe that such circumstances were normal. It's astonishing how one can gradually start to perceive something so traumatic as ordinary or even acceptable over time. When you find yourself deeply traumatized, your mind enters a state of survival, leaving you unable to think or reason. It's a complex process that many people struggle to comprehend fully.

On a scorching mid-summer afternoon, Alex returned home from work looking visibly upset, as if burdened by something. Concerned about his well-being, I approached him and asked what was bothering him. However, he remained silent, his troubled thoughts evident as he paced restlessly in the living room.

Seeing him like this, I was genuinely worried. I watched him as he made several phone calls, each conversation adding to the tension in the room. Soon, cars pulled up outside our home. Moments later, his parents and sister entered the room, their faces reflecting concern and determination. It became clear that something was about to happen.

"Anna, come here," his father requested, his voice carrying a sense of gravity that made my heart skip a beat.

Curious about what was happening, I approached, my anticipation growing with each step.

"Ask her, Alex," his mother said. "You have the right to know."

Alex stood up and approached me, his eyes filled with rage. He demanded to know every detail of the coffee meetup with a colleague I had at Starbucks that Wednesday evening.

Suppressing a nervous laugh, I maintained my composure and calmly clarified the situation. "He's just a colleague from work, nothing more. We had to collaborate on an important report." Little did I know that my response would trigger an unimaginable chain of events.

Alex's anger escalated to an alarming level. He hurled a barrage of insults at me, his words cutting through the air like daggers. I was shocked and terrified. I never expected things to escalate to this extent. In a horrifying turn of events, Alex's anger transformed into physical violence. I felt the sharp pain as his fist connected with my face, resulting in a broken nose and painful bruises.

Summoning all the strength I had left, both physically and emotionally, I rose to my feet. Something within me shifted. Without uttering a single word, I decided to remove myself from the toxic situation.

I retreated to my bedroom and gathered a few essential belongings: my wallet, my certificates, and my car keys. As I left the confines of that house, I made a conscious decision never to look back.

It took six arduous months, but finally, the divorce proceedings came to an end.

***

Now, the group stood up and applauded.

"Congratulations, Anna," Dr. Kathy exclaimed. "You are an intelligent and resilient woman."

Anna quickly corrected her. "It wasn't me, but Krishna, who deserves the credit. I heard a small voice deep within that whispered, "My sweet Anna, leave." It was Krishna.

It was an emotional evening. The group came together for a group hug. With a cheerful exclamation, Dr. Kathy bid farewell.

As they parted ways, rain began to fall. Anna, without an umbrella, let the raindrops fall on her freely, and this time, she wasn't crying in the rain.

Five

"He's more myself than I am. Whatever our souls are made of, his and mine are the same."

— Emily Brontë, Wuthering Heights

As she continued walking in the rain, a black car pulled up behind her. It was John. "Anna, need a ride home?" he offered, flashing a warm smile.

Anna hesitated for a moment, then thought, *why not?* She settled into the front seat next to him.

"Anna, I thought your story was so powerful!" John said.

Anna smiled. "Hope you will find some inspiration from it."

With a smile on his face, he continued to drive. Anna couldn't help but admire John's salt-and-pepper grey hair, sharp jawline, and athletic physique. He exuded an irresistible charm that made Anna feel an unexpected wave of desire. "I love your cologne! What's is it?"

He chuckled and replied, "It's called Amouage Journey,"

As their eyes met, Anna's legs felt weak, and a surge of emotions engulfed her. *This can't be real,* she thought. *What on earth is happening?* With each passing mile, Anna's inner monologue grew louder. *This is so strange; I've never experienced anything like this before.* The desire to touch his hand consumed her, and at that moment, John reached out and interlocked their fingers, never missing a beat while driving.

After a short drive, they arrived at Anna's residence. She stepped out of the car and thanked him for his kindness. Just as John was about to drive away, Anna turned, a mischievous glint in her eyes, and asked, "How about some spicy tea?"

John's heart skipped a beat, his eagerness real. He parked his car and caught up with her, their hands interlocking as they strolled towards her door. Anna unlocked it and guided John inside. As soon as they stepped foot in the house, John couldn't restrain himself. With a hunger he didn't know he possessed, he pulled her close, and their lips met in a passionate kiss. Anna melted into his arms, returning his desire with equal fervor.

Anna was shocked at her own response. First, she got into a car with John, and now she was kissing him. She quickly pulled away. "This isn't me. I don't know what happened. I am so sorry, John," she said.

John looked equally embarrassed himself. "I'll see you at the meeting next Saturday," he mumbled before hastily leaving her house.

John arrived home and immediately gave Noah a warm hug. All through the evening, he had a nervous energy about him. He sat for dinner and began to compliment Martha, which was unusual. John tasted the meal and exclaimed, "Martha, this is amazing! I love this dish".

Later, in the shower, as the water flowed gently down his body, John's thoughts drifted to the unexpected kiss with Anna. It had left a lingering sensation, a sexual awakening, and he let it flow unrestrained.

Anna retired to bed, donning the dress with traces of John's cologne. The scent comforted and excited her. Unconcerned with its implications or what lay ahead, she embraced the present moment, fully immersed in its enchantment. "Goodnight, John," she whispered. "Who are you, really? Another soul mate? Another lifetime?"

Six

"Love looks not with the eyes, but with the mind,

And therefore, is winged Cupid painted blind."

— William Shakespeare,

That Saturday, the sky was filled with dark clouds, and the rain poured relentlessly. In the distance, you could hear thunder rumbling, and now and then, the sky lit up with flashes of lightning. Martha looked at John and said, "You really shouldn't go out today, John. The weather's pretty awful."

"I have to go," John responded. "Don't worry, I'll be fine." He knew today was the day he had to share his story, and nothing could deter him. His heart yearned to see Anna, as he wanted to share his story with her more than anyone else.

When he arrived at Dr. Kathy's place, an eerie silence greeted him. Dr. Kathy eventually emerged. "Do you think anyone else will brave this weather to join us?" John pondered aloud, his voice filled with uncertainty.

Dr. Kathy's response was far from reassuring. "Maybe not, but let's give it a little more time, shall we?"

As they waited, John's heart raced with anticipation. *What if no one showed up? What if Anna failed to make an appearance?*

Amid a torrential downpour, Anna emerged, drenched to the bone. Her form-fitting gown clung to her, accentuating her attractive silhouette. Every strand of her hair glistened with raindrops, cascading like delicate petals. John found himself unable to tear his gaze away from her captivating presence.

"Hmm, there's a message from Jake and Lilly. They won't be able to make it to the gathering tonight. Apologies, but we'll have to reschedule this much-anticipated get-together for next Saturday." Understanding the disappointment that lingered in the room, Kathy quickly suggested, "Why don't we all take a moment to dry ourselves off and gather around the cozy fireplace? I'll prepare a comforting cup of hot tea for us to savor before your departure."

Dr. Kathy noticed a glimmer of appreciation in John and Anna's eyes as they exchanged a heartfelt look. They nodded in agreement, grateful for the warmth and hospitality offered on this rainy evening, but hurriedly stepped out into the rain-soaked world. John swung open the car door, a grin spreading across his face as Anna climbed in. "I was so worried you wouldn't show up." John couldn't help but say it.

Anna's mischievous smile danced in response, and at that moment, their connection deepened.

As they stepped into Anna's apartment, Anna handed John a towel to dry himself. "I'm a good cook, you know. Would you like to stay for dinner?"

"What are you cooking, girl?" he asked, unable to hide his curiosity.

With a twinkle in her eyes, she responded, "I can grill some mouthwatering chicken tandoori and whip up a fresh salad. We can enjoy it with warm Rotis."

John's stomach growled in anticipation. "Sounds delicious," he exclaimed, unable to contain his hunger."

Anna took the marinated tandoori pieces and carefully placed them on a tray, switching on the grill. John sat at the kitchen table, his eyes fixated on her every move.

"I am looking forward to hearing your story, John," Anna said as she continued to cut the vegetables for the salad.

"Oh, Anna, don't worry! We have next Saturday to catch up. So, what are your plans for the rest of the week?

"Work, work, and more work," sighed Anna. "But you know what? I was hoping you could give me some cooking classes. The only catch is that you'll have to go grocery shopping with me at the local store.

With a grin, John replied, "Sure thing! And I'll take you to my favorite organic farmers' market store. That's where I saw the notice about joining this amazing group. How about you?"

"My co-worker is friends with Dr. Kathy, and she mentioned that Dr. Kathy hosts these group meetings that are not only beneficial but also combine elements of spirituality. It's not just about concrete science, and I jumped at the opportunity to be a part of it", Anna said as she continued the cooking.

"Are you religious?" John asked curiously.

"No. I am spiritual."

"What does that mean?"

Anna pondered for a moment before answering. "It means that there are many things we don't know. Yet, we understand that all living beings are intricately connected to the divine source."

He seemed surprised. "You are not a Hindu, are you?"

Chuckling softly, Anna responded, "No, John. I was raised as a Christian."

"Do you believe in reincarnation?" John asked.

"Maybe. Perhaps one life is not enough to balance all the karmas," Anna replied.

Dinner was finally ready, and they sat down to eat. As Anna reached for a piece of chicken with her bare hands, she turned to John with a smile and asked, "Do you mind if I eat with my hands?"

John was captivated by Anna's carefree spirit. "I would love to join you!" He watched in awe as Anna effortlessly tore pieces of tender chicken, added a generous portion of salad, and skillfully rolled it up in a warm roti. "You make it look so easy, Anna," John remarked, unable to hide his admiration.

Anna playfully offered John a bite.

"Now you're feeding me," John teased, his eyes welling up with emotion.

"Just like your mom," Anna whispered.

For a brief moment, silence enveloped the room as Anna caught a glimpse of what seemed like tears in John's eyes. But he quickly brushed them away, not wanting to spoil the joyous atmosphere they had created.

"Did I say something wrong?" Anna asked, feeling a tinge of worry.

. "Next Saturday," he declared, "when I unveil my story, everything will become clear. Can you wait?"

Anna's reassuring response echoed with sincerity, "Take all the time you want."

John gathered his bag and left.

Anna couldn't help but reflect on what a stunning evening it had been. Just before John left, he made sure to exchange numbers, hinting at a future grocery shopping date.

Seven

"There is no remedy for love but to love more."

-Victor Hugo

It was a Wednesday evening, and John found himself in a race against time to conclude his meetings. Desperately seeking the last papers he needed to sign before calling it a day, he turned to his secretary, Hallie. Much to her amusement, Hallie had noticed a remarkable transformation in John lately. There was a newfound sparkle in his eyes, a constant smile adorning his face, and an unmistakable aura of liveliness surrounding him.

Intrigued by this mysterious change, she cautiously approached him and whispered, "What's the rush, John? Do you have a hot date?"

Caught off guard by her inquiry, John's eyes widened, and he replied, "Not exactly, just felt like, you know, going home and watching a movie??

"Really?" Hallie said. "Hmm. I can smell something that is off the charts!"

"Come on, Hallie," John said, "you've known me for so many years!"

John signed off on all his documents for the day and then swiftly made his way to the restroom. He changed into a pair of fashionable jeans and a crisp white shirt, leaving the top buttons undone to show a bit of his bronzed chest. As a final touch, he sprayed on his favorite cologne and made his way to his car.

He started his car, his fingers fumbling with excitement. He picked up his phone and texted Anna, "Anna, I'm on my way. Let's meet at the school, and then we can go and get our groceries." He received a thumbs-up from Anna.

Anna donned a breathtaking white dress adorned with delicate ruffles gracefully cascading down her arms. A magnetic aura of vibrant energy surrounded her, drawing him in. They drove to the organic store.

"Anna, you have to taste these! Trust me, once you try these, the stuff we get from the regular grocery store will taste like garbage," John said confidently.

"John, not everyone can afford those high prices, you know? Personally, I just wash my regular veggies with vinegar and water to get rid of those pesky pesticides. Works like a charm!"

John laughed. "You're right! I guess I can be a bit of an expensive shopper sometimes," he said, brushing his hand through her hair affectionately. "Let's get what we need here and then go to the regular grocery store for the rest!"

Anna went and got enough produce for a salad, and she picked up some salmon to bake.

"Back home, we grow all our veggies, and they taste very different, John. You know, the ones we pick from the garden." Anna was silent for a minute, then added, "It's been a while, and sometimes I really miss my mom's home-cooked food."

With a curious look in his eyes, John turned to Anna and asked, "Have you ever gone back?"

Anna's face softened as she replied, "Nope! My folks weren't exactly thrilled about my divorce. It was a tough time for the whole family, and they were so concerned about their reputation. They thought I didn't put enough effort into making my marriage work." Anna paused for a moment, her voice filled with a mix of sadness and anger, "They even asked me not to come back home because they were focused on finding a good match for my sister. They were afraid my divorce would affect her chances of getting good proposals."

John, with a touch of sympathy, responded, "It's challenging, Anna. I apologize."

Anna nodded, her eyes filled with a sense of acceptance. "Yes, it is what it is," she said. "But you know, if I had stayed, I think I would have just given up. My heart and body would have simply given up!"

John gently squeezed her hand, a comforting gesture that spoke volumes.

"I have no complaints," Anna said with a smile. "There's this incredible book I've been reading, and it's like a revelation. It took me from questioning 'why did this happen to me?' to embracing the realization that it all had to happen."

As they arrived home, Anna wasted no time washing the produce with vinegar and water before marinating the salmon. "White wine?" she asked John with a mischievous smile.

"Absolutely," he replied, raising his glass. "Here's to us and to Dr. Kathy for all her help."

"We shouldn't be hanging out like this, John," Anna said, a hint of concern in her voice.

John looked at her, his eyes sparkling with excitement. "Sometimes, Anna, you have to break the rules if it feels right! What was the book you were talking about in the car?"

"It's a book that delves into the purpose of our existence on Earth," Anna replied.

"According to the book, Earth is like a school, and we are here to learn valuable life lessons. It suggests that before coming here, we chose our own life and the specific lessons that would aid our growth and development. It emphasizes the importance of being in human form to truly grasp these lessons. And the most intriguing part is that we have multiple lives, reincarnating until we master the teachings. But, John, we are not alone on this journey. We have guides and angels who support us every step of the way. Trust me, this book is truly fascinating, and I'm learning so much from it!"

"Very interesting, Anna. I am not sure about multiple lives or even eternal life. I think once this human life is over, we are done. I mean, we get recycled into some tree. I didn't mean to offend you, darling," John laughed with affection written all over his face.

Anna paused for a moment and then continued. "We all have soul mates, John. Some enter our lives to propel us towards important lessons, serving as our teachers along the way. Others come to offer healing and support. Soul mates can take on various roles - friends, siblings, romantic partners, parents, teachers, or mentors. When we view it from this perspective, we may realize that even if someone has hurt us, it might have been necessary to awaken us. It's not entirely their fault, or maybe it is to some extent. After all, we all have free will and the power to choose. Perhaps they could have still taught us the lesson without causing pain, but who knows? Ultimately, we can't prove any of these theories!"

"I guess so," said John, walking behind Anna and burying his face in her hair. "Dinner ready, babe?" John asked.

Anna arranged the table, presenting John with fresh salad and blackened salmon. After dinner, they nestled by the warm, crackling fire. In an affectionate embrace, he drew her near, savoring the intimacy of the moment. Gently, he brushed his lips against her neck, igniting a spark of desire. With a tantalizing touch, he caressed every curve of her face and neck, igniting Anna's deepest desires. Slowly and gently, she began to unbutton his shirt. She buried her face in his chest, kissing him with deep affection and passion. John looked at her and then gently held her face. "Anna, are you still in love with Krishna?" he asked.

Anna met John's gaze and replied, "Yes, I adore him, but it's not the fiery passion of romantic love. I don't feel the need to search him out, hunt him down, and plead for a second chance.

Instead, it's the gentle presence of him in my heart, blossoming from that teenage infatuation into an unwavering source of strength." She whispered, emphasizing, "He is not your competition in any way!"

John's smile widened as he pulled her closer, their lips meeting in a passionate kiss. It was as if their desire had intensified, igniting a fire within them. With a gentle exploration, he parted her lips, his tongue eagerly intertwining with hers. The intensity grew as she reciprocated. At that moment, they were transported to a world of their own.

As they kissed, Anna's lips' softness and sweetness were drawing John in like a bee to nectar. His mouth moved hungrily against hers, each kiss a delicious exploration of desire. Their tongues knotted in a fleshly ballet, swapping the flavors of passion and longing.

Anna's warm and inviting breath caressed John's cheek as he pressed closer, deepening their kiss. Her delicate moans, like a melody of pleasure, ignited the fire within him. Their connection was electric, every moment filled with an insatiable hunger for each other.

John's hands, filled with the intoxicating scent of Anna's hair, cupped her face, holding her gently yet firmly. Their mouths moved with a pulse all their own, a work of art — of desire — that resonated through the room. It was as though time had stopped, leaving only the two of them lost in the raw intensity of the moment.

Their hands roamed freely, exploring the contours of each other's bodies. John's fingertips traced the curve of Anna's waist, sending electric shivers down her spine. Her delicate touch, in return, set his skin ablaze with appetite. Their breaths coordinated, their hearts pounding in unison as they lost themselves in the intoxicating time of their physical need.

Anna's fingers entwined with John's hair, pulling him closer as they developed their piecing together. Their mouths explored every inch, igniting a fire that seemed insatiable. Soft whimpers of pleasure escaped their lips, peppering the bodily concerto of their lovemaking.

With a gentle yet pressing urgency, John's hand moved down the curve of Anna's back, tracing the delicate line of her spine.

"Ahh," the woman moaned the loudest this time. His touch left a trail of goosebumps in its wake, and Anna arched into him, a silent plea for more. He obliged, his fingers expertly dancing along the curves of her bulk, kindling a wish that was now almost unbearable to delay.

As their bodies pressed together, they surrendered. They gave up on the climaxing peak of the undeniable chemistry that had brought them together.

Anna's fingers traced the broad expanse of John's shoulders, reveling in the strength of his cuddle. John, in turn, worshipped every edge of her with his indulgent trace.

Amidst their shared thirst, their eyes locked, and they exchanged silent words of lust and devotion. The strength of their linking grew with each passing second, and it was as though the world had worn away, leaving only the two of them in a land of love.

Their lovemaking was a tender dance, a beautiful and passionate culmination of their shared feelings. Each movement, each stroke, spoke of their unfathomable fondness and pining for one another. Their figures stimulated in agreement, a piece of music that echoed through the room but silently.

Amidst their passionate entwining, the fervor of their connection escalated to a point of no return. Their bodies moved together, each thrust intensifying the magnetic pull between them. Every force was harder than the previous one. With every powerful shove of craving, they drew closer to their shared climax, the finale of their profound union.

As their bodies reached the peak of ecstasy, they quivered, attached to each other. A crescendo of pleasure that left them both gasping for breath. In the ensuing aftermath, their hearts beat loudly; the room was filled with a stillness that bore witness to the gravity of their release.

As the waves of pleasure washed over them, they held each other in the afterglow, their hearts and souls intertwined. The soft, post-lovemaking pecks they shared were filled with tenderness and reassurance. In the quiet instants following their joint climax, John and Anna found solace in each other's arms. Their naked bodies nestled together, wrapped in the warmth of their intimate connection.

John's strong arms enveloped Anna, cradling her as if she were the most precious treasure in the world. John cradled her with a tender strength that made her feel cherished and secure. Her head snuggled against his broad chest; her ear pressed to the soothing beat of his heartbeat, which reverberated through her like a comforting lullaby. She could feel the rise and fall of his chest with each slow and steady breath, and it synchronized perfectly with her own.

Her body molded to his, every curve fitting seamlessly against his form. His hands caressed her back, his fingers tracing a delicate path along her spine, sending down subdued shivers. Her fingertips lightly traced the silhouettes of his muscular shoulders, her touch imbued with an unspoken desire to convey her affection.

Their legs intertwined, creating an intimate connection that went beyond words. Anna could feel the warmth of John's skin against her own, their bodies melding together as if they were meant to be one. It was a moment of intimacy, a beautiful testament to the love that had blossomed between them.

As they lay there, swathed in each other's arms, their whispered words of affection and dreams continued to fill the air, deepening their connection with each passing moment. In the quietude of the night, they found completeness, two souls matted in a love that knew no confines.

Their post-lovemaking cuddles were tender, a silent declaration of their longing for each other while the room was bathed in the soft glow of moonlight, casting a mild aura around them.

With a contented sigh, John pressed a loving kiss to Anna's forehead, his lips lingering there for a moment. "You are absolutely amazing, Anna," he murmured, his voice filled with adoration.

They lay there in the tranquility of the night, lost in each other's clasp, the world outside fading into insignificance.

Eight

"The supreme happiness in life is the conviction that we are loved."

Leo Tolstoy

Dr. Kathy eagerly prepared the room for the session, reminiscing about how long it had been since the last one. The scent of her freshly baked ginger cookies wafted through the air, accompanied by a refreshing concoction of gooseberry and lime.

Jake, breaking away from his usual scrubs, was the first to arrive, dressed in a black shirt and blue jeans. He poured a glass of the tangy gooseberry juice and settled comfortably on the mat. Soon after, Lilly entered, taking a seat next to Jake. Despite being the youngest in the group, she exuded a maturity well beyond her years. As John and Anna hadn't arrived yet, the session had to be delayed.

Curiosity getting the best of him, Jake turned to Lilly and asked, "Are you in college?"

"I would love to go to college, Jake, but it's just not financially feasible for me right now," Lilly confessed. "I'm saving up, though, hoping to become a medical assistant in the future."

"Why not consider taking a loan?" Jake suggested.

A hint of disappointment clouded Lilly's face. "My credit scores aren't great," she admitted. "But I'm working on improving them. I'm focusing on saving money and paying off all my debts."

Jake's gaze lingered on Lilly, witnessing her determination and dreams. "Lilly, I have clinics on Saturdays. If you're interested, you can come and work as my medical support assistant on weekends. It'll help you save up that extra penny for college. You have basic computer skills, right?"

Lilly's joy was palpable as she nodded.

John walked in next and quickly scanned the room for Anna. He then sat right next to Jake, keeping some distance between them. Anna came in last, and after greeting everyone, she sat down next to Lilly. John and Anna made it a point to avoid each other.

Dr. Kathy walked in and started the group with a calming meditation. Afterward, she asked, "Who's going next?"

John spoke up. "It's my turn!" He hesitated for a moment, lost in thought or perhaps searching for the right words. It took him a while to gather his thoughts and find the courage to begin his story, but eventually, he managed to piece his words together.

"I don't even know who my parents are. I don't even know how I got this surname. I was in the system and raised by CYS, and I spent my whole childhood moving from one foster home to another.

My earliest memory was when I was around five years old. I had this little bag with my clothes, and this CYS social worker took me in her car and dropped me off at this foster home. That's when I met my first foster mom. She was such a sweet lady, kind-hearted. Her house was super tiny, out in the country, and she already had four other foster kids she looked after. When she saw me, she came out and hugged me. She must have been in her 60s or something.

At first, I was petrified and hesitant to open up. I had been through a lot, and there were times when I felt like no one would ever want me. But after spending some time with her, I started to feel safe again. She never once judged me or made me feel like I was unacceptable. She was like a mother to me, and I really loved her.

But soon enough, things changed again. My social worker returned and told me that she had found a permanent home for me. She also said that the foster mom wouldn't be able to care for me anymore as she was getting too old. So, I had to leave the only place I've ever called home.

When it was time for me to leave my first foster home, man, I was heartbroken. I put on this brave face, hugged my foster mom, and said goodbye with a smile. But deep down, I was shattered. I cried my eyes out for days when I was alone, I'm telling you. I went through these dark moments where I didn't even want to eat. I felt abandoned, alone, like I wasn't worth anything. I missed my foster mom but didn't have anyone to share those feelings with.

My next foster home was supposed to be the one, you know? The permanent one. But then my second foster mom, who wanted to adopt me, got sick with this terminal illness. Life just wasn't fair. And so, they took me away again. By then, I was a teenager, and no family wanted to adopt me. So, it became this pattern of being shuffled from one home to another. And you know what? I got used to it. I started living in each home without getting attached to anyone. I didn't even know what it meant to have a close bond with someone. I kept to myself and focused on my studies. I was good in school, and that's how I managed to get this scholarship to college. And that's how I survived and became independent.

But let me tell you, college was tough. I was a loner. People thought I was a bit weird. I mostly kept to myself. After college, I started my own business, and here I am today.

I think I'll forever be known as the one who graduated college with a degree and still had my virginity intact", John laughed.

"You got a fine sense of humor, John." Lilly loved John's comment about his intact virginity.

Anna smiled at John and looked away.

"Ok, let me finish my story," said John, and continued.

"My business skyrocketed, launching me into a realm of newfound luck and opportunity. During this time, I crossed paths with beautiful aspiring models, including my ex-wife, Anastasia. Her beauty was simply breathtaking, and her drive matched her ambition. With captivating light eyes and a physique that belonged on the runway, she stood out from the crowd. Although our conversations were limited due to language issues, you know, she spoke Russian and knew little English, our physical connection was nothing short of extraordinary". A mischievous smile crept across John's face.

She was the only woman I had ever known, so I proposed to her. At first, she wasn't interested, but one day, she expressed her desire to marry me. Later, I discovered she was facing financial struggles and couldn't afford her rent. We decided to get married in court, and she moved into my home. However, she made it clear that she wouldn't give up on her dream of becoming a supermodel.

One day, while I was at work, Anastasia urgently called me in a state of distress. She was sobbing on the phone and insisted that I rush home due to an emergency. When I arrived, I found her sitting on the bed, devastated. She looked at me with sadness and disgust and said, "John, it's terrible... I'm pregnant. I want to terminate this pregnancy."

She repeated, "I don't want this thing. I don't want this thing. Can you please remove it?"

I gently responded, "Darling, it's not a thing. It's our baby."

She continued crying. We had numerous heated arguments about it and one day, I presented her with a choice: keep the baby and stay with me or go your own way. Ultimately, she decided to keep the baby.

Afterward, she underwent a drastic change. Her radiant smile vanished, her words ceased, and she began to view me as her adversary, who shattered her dreams. Hostility consumed her, and she started to sleep in a separate bed.

I accompanied her to all her appointments, but her speech dwindled to a mere whisper. Eventually, she gave birth to Noah and didn't even want to look at him. When the doctor disclosed that he had Down syndrome, she couldn't stop screaming, "It's all your fault!"

Concerned about her well-being, I suggested counseling for possible postpartum depression, but she declined. Surprisingly, she agreed to join a gym and hired a personal trainer. Eventually, she mentioned a new modeling assignment in France, appearing genuinely happy. However, a week later, I received a divorce petition from her. In the petition, she granted me full custody of Noah and requested that neither of us ever contact her again.

Once more, I found myself deserted and left behind!

John stood there, tears streaming down his face like a waterfall, tracing paths of sorrow on his cheeks. With a gentle touch, Anna placed a box of tissues in his trembling hands.

Meanwhile, Lilly's heart, resonating with compassion, rose gracefully from her seat. When she reached him, she enveloped him in a tight, comforting hug.

Lost in a sea of introspection, Jake lowered his gaze.

"My story is far from over," John declared. "Without my child, who was sent to guide and heal me, I would have lived a life oblivious to the true meaning of love. He has Down syndrome, and all he knows is to love unconditionally, and he will never abandon me. I am sure Noah was sent to heal me."

As the session ended, everyone bid their farewells and exited the room. John made his way to his car, opened the door, and sat down quietly. Anna followed closely behind, slipping into the passenger seat. The two of them drove off in silence, their words unspoken but understood.

Nine

"I love you because the entire universe conspired to help me find you."

— Paul Coelho, The Alchemist

Having dinner with Anna has become a regular thing now. They both walked into her apartment, holding hands. Anna opened the door, went to the fridge, and returned with a glass of water for John. She held his hand and asked him gently, "Are you okay?"

All John could utter was a feeble "Not really" before his emotions overwhelmed him. Collapsing to his knees, he unleashed the flood of sorrow and trauma inside him. Anna held him in her arms as she would hold a fragile child. Holding his tear-stained face against her bosom, she whispered, "I'm here for you, my love. Let it all out." With tender strokes of his hair and gentle caresses on his face, they remained entwined on the floor.

In the stillness of the apartment, John and Anna's conversations dug deeper into the crux of their growing relationship. They found themselves drawn to each other, their souls intertwining as they shared their hopes, dreams, and fears.

As they sat together on the couch, John turned to Anna with a contemplative expression. "You know, Anna," he began, "your presence in my life has been like a ray of sunshine breaking through the darkest clouds. I never expected to find someone who would understand me so deeply, who would be there to catch me when I fell apart."

Anna gazed into his eyes with a tender smile. "John, you've also brought so much light into my life," she replied. "Your resilience and strength inspire me every day. I feel like we're on this incredible journey together, discovering the depths of our connection and understanding."

Their hands found each other, fingers interlocking as they continued to share their innermost thoughts. John's voice softened as he said, "I used to be so guarded, afraid to let anyone in. But with you, Anna, it's different. I want to open up, I want to share my world with you, and I want to be there for you in every way I can."

Anna leaned in, brushing her lips against his in a tender kiss. "John, I feel the same way," she whispered. "With you, I've learned to let go of my past and embrace the present moment."

He traced his finger along her cheek. "You have the most beautiful smile. It's like the only happiness in my life."

Her cheeks flushed as she responded, "And your laughter, it's my favorite melody. It fills my heart with joy every time."

Their hands twisted, he confessed, "I never believed in destiny, but meeting you feels like fate intervened to bring us together."

She smiled warmly, "It's as if the universe conspired to lead us to each other. I'm grateful for every twist and turn that brought us here."

His voice hushed to a whisper as he said, "I love the way your eyes light up when you talk about your dreams. You have this incredible passion, and it's contagious."

Their foreheads touched as she replied, "And you, your determination and strength inspire me to be a better person every day. You make me believe in myself."

His lips brushed against her neck, and he murmured, "You're my safe haven. When I'm with you, all the chaos and pain in the world fade away, and it's just us."

She closed her eyes, savoring the moment. "You're my anchor. With you, I feel like I can weather any storm that life throws our way."

Their conversations were not just words; they were love letters exchanged in the quiet moments, affirmations of a love deepening with each passing day. In the balminess of their love, they found relief, hope, and a promise of forever.

As their kisses deepened, their connection grew stronger, and they knew they were falling in love with each other, not just with the idea of love itself. Each conversation, each shared moment, brought them closer to a love that was destined to endure.

Their relationship continued to evolve like a beautiful symphony playing out the melodies of their hearts. With each passing day, they discovered new facets of each other.

In the deep embrace of the night, their solace was shattered by the persistent ringing of John's phone. Reluctantly, he disentangled himself from Anna's embrace, uttering a heartfelt "Thank you, Anna." Martha was calling, reminding him of home and Noah's waiting presence. As Anna smiled and accompanied him to the car, their farewell was sealed with a lingering kiss. It was a kiss that transcended the physical, forging a spiritual and soulful connection between them.

Anna retired to her bed and laid down, and a newfound realization struck her — she was now in love with John.

As John entered his home, he was greeted by Noah, who rushed towards him, falling into his loving embrace. John lifted Noah in his arms, showering him with kisses. With a heart brimming with boundless love, he continued to express his affection, whispering, "Noah, I love you" repeatedly.

During dinner time, the air was filled with lively conversations and laughter. Martha couldn't help but notice the transformation in John as well. Whatever was causing this shift, she thought, it was a positive change.

As John settled into bed, he felt a weight lifted off his shoulders that he hadn't experienced in years. With a heart at peace, free from the burdens of past traumas, he drifted into a deep and restful sleep.

The next day, he sent a message to Anna saying, "Hey Anna, I have this weekend off from work. If you're available, there's a beautiful hillside resort where we can spend our weekend together. I'll also get Noah and Martha. It's the perfect place to relax and recharge. Let me know your thoughts."

Anna was more than happy. She started to look forward to the weekend.

On the weekend, they took a road trip to a serene countryside inn, just a two-hour drive from New York City. As night fell, Martha accompanied Noah and retired to bed.

John and Anna then cuddled up in front of the cozy fireplace, watching as the flames danced and crackled.

John's heart raced as he knew the time had arrived for THE conversation. "Anna," he whispered, "I love you. Can you imagine sharing your life with me? I understand the gravity of this decision, and I don't expect an immediate answer."

Anna was silent for some time, then said, "It's not that I don't love you, but I need to trust myself first. Can we take it one day at a time without any promises for tomorrow? I've been hurt, and it will take time for me to trust again to accept love. I doubt love, even though I yearn to both receive and give it." Her words trailed off, a hint of vulnerability in her voice. "I hope you understand," she stammered.

"I understand," John said, his voice laced with desire as he lovingly took Anna's hand.

With a gentle tug, he led her to the bedroom.

The room was bathed in a soft, golden glow, the curtains drawn just enough to allow the moonlight to filter in, casting a romantic spell. The air was scented with a subtle hint of vanilla and roses, a fragrance that promised sensuality.

The bed was a vision of temptation. It was huge, adorned with a delicate scattering of velvety rose petals, their deep red hues contrasting beautifully against the pristine white sheets. Soft, quixotic music played in the background, melodic notes adding to the seductive mood.

Anna wore a silk robe that clung to her every curve, the fabric a tantalizing whisper against her skin. Her eyes met John's with a mixture of need and vulnerability, and her lips slightly parted in suspense and willingness. She felt like a goddess, ready to be worshipped by the man who had ignited a fire within her.

John's attire was in the same way alluring, his shirt unbuttoned just enough to reveal the outlines of his chest and his jeans fitting snugly. His gaze bore into Anna's with an intensity that awakened her sensuality. He was a man on a mission, determined to explore every inch of her with his hands and lips.

As they stood there, the chemistry between them crackled in the air. John's fingers brushed against Anna's cheek; his touch feather-light yet electric. He leaned in, capturing her lips in a searing kiss that left no room for doubt about his intentions. Their tongues danced in a passionate tango, each kiss deepening their connection.

The foreplay was a sluggish, tantalizing survey of each other's bodies and their requests. John's hands traced a path down Anna's physique, his fingers igniting spurs of pleasure wherever they touched. Anna's soft sighs filled the room as she arched against him, her body responding to his every stroke.

With each passing moment, their craving grew, a passionate crescendo threatening to consume them both. The bed beckoned, a haven for their love to unfold. As they finally succumbed to its inviting embrace, they knew that this night would be an opus of need, a proof of the love that bound them together.

As the night deepened, their playful teasing gave way to a seductive dance of desire and longing. Their bodies moved together in an intricate rhythm, each touch and caress igniting the flames of their passion. John's lips whispered erotic abilities against Anna's skin, making her tremble with keenness.

In the early hours of the morning, with the soft light of dawn filtering through the curtains, they lay entangled in a sensual reverie, their bodies still electric with the memory of their lovemaking. John's eyes held a mischievous glint as he gazed at Anna. "You, Anna," he purred, "are a temptation I can never resist."

Anna's fingers traced teasing patterns on his chest, her voice a sultry purr. "And you, John," she whispered, "have a way of making me crave more every time."

With a final, lingering kiss filled with possibilities of more to come, they surrendered to the blissful exhaustion of their desires.

As they lay there, the world outside ceased to exist, and time seemed to stand still. The soft, rhythmic cadence of their breaths filled the room, harmonizing in a wordless symphony of love and contentment. John gazed into the depths of Anna's eyes, his heart beating in tandem with hers, the connection between them transcending mere physicality.

Anna's fingers traced delicate patterns on John's back, her touch both soothing and electrifying. She marveled at the strength of the emotions coursing through her, a torrent of desire, tenderness, and longing. With a soft smile, she whispered words of affection that hung in the air like a fragrant perfume, filling the room with their sweetness.

John, his face nuzzled against the crook of Anna's neck, inhaled her scent, committing it to memory. He murmured words of love and devotion, his voice a gentle caress against her skin. The night had been a whirlwind of passion and playfulness, but in this quiet moment, they basked in the afterglow, savoring the profound connection they had forged.

Their love was a journey worth indulging in, promising a future filled with playful laughter, tender moments, and passionate embraces. As they succumbed to the sweet embrace of sleep, their souls remained intertwined, their hearts beating in harmony, leaving them yearning for the next chapter of their enticing adventure, a journey of love that held the promise of infinite tomorrows.

They knew their love was a journey worth indulging in, one playful and passionate day at a time. As they succumbed to the sweet embrace of sleep, their connection deepened, leaving them yearning for the next chapter of their enticing adventure.

Ten

"The only thing that can make you happy is yourself."

- Aristotle

On the third Saturday, fate wove its intricate web, unveiling a web of secrets. Little did anyone know, Anna and John had embarked on a clandestine romance hidden from prying eyes. Seated at opposite ends, their stolen glances spoke volumes, a silent dance of longing. They yearned to keep their love under the radar.

Lilly diligently worked as an MSA in Jake's office on Saturdays, determined to save money for her education. Dr. Kathy, with her usual warmth, started the session with a meditation. The soothing music guided them to focus on their breath and direct their awareness to their heart space. There, a golden flame flickered in their mind's eye, expanding beyond their physical existence, reaching out to the vastness of the universe. As the divine energy merged with the golden beam, Dr. Kathy encouraged them to anchor this divinity into their flame — a transformative expansion of consciousness. Through this journey, she guided them to cultivate a self-concept rooted in love, abundance, self-confidence, and self-respect.

Then, with a warm smile, she went around the room, carefully handing out freshly baked chocolate muffins that were still warm to the touch. She also distributed glasses of refreshing pomegranate juice.

Just when everyone thought it would be a simple storytelling session, Dr. Kathy, the master of surprises, took it up a notch. She started passing out beautifully bound journals to each person in the room. The covers were adorned with intricate designs.

She handed each person a pen and encouraged them to write down their short-term goals, those little steps that would pave the way for personal growth and self-transformation. But she didn't stop there. She wanted them to dream big, to envision their long-term goals, the aspirations that would shape their lives.

As the room fell into a comfortable silence, she challenged them to explore the depths of their emotions. Starting with happiness, she asked them to close their eyes and recall moments of pure joy, capturing those fleeting feelings in words. The energy in the room shifted as they moved on to more complex emotions like anger, shame, and hurt, each person delving into their own experiences with vulnerability and honesty.

At that moment, surrounded by the aroma of chocolate muffins, the taste of pomegranate juice, and the power of written words, a sense of anticipation filled the air. Each person held their pen, ready to embark on a journey of self-discovery, armed with the tools to transform their lives, one word at a time.

Kathy said, "I'll take a quick look at all your definitions of the emotions and read out loud a few that might be inspiring".

John was deep in thought, holding his pen, imagining a life filled with love that never abandons you. He defined happiness as a place in one's life where a love that never leaves lives and never dies.

Anna penned the word "happiness," and beneath it, she sketched a picture. It came alive with a small cabin house nestled by the sparkling sea. Outside, a loving family tended to their garden as the sun dipped below the mighty blue waves, painting the sky in vibrant hues.

Jake wrote: "Happiness is found in exploring exotic locations, savoring the finest cuisine, cruising in luxury cars, and building multiple streams of income."

Lilly wrote: "Own a small store one day, filled with canned food and non-perishable items, always ready to lend a hand to those in need. For me, true happiness means taking care of others and spreading kindness."

Dr. Kathy instructed them to read their writings aloud, followed by a question-and-answer session. During this time, Lilly was the sole participant who posed a question to Jake.

She asked, "Jake, you already have everything you just wrote. So, why are you here?"

Jake said, "I have them, and yes, I get them, and I feel good for a while, but then I start feeling empty again. I'm here because I want to find something that lasts forever, something that can fill the void inside of me. That's what true happiness means to me."

Dr. Kathy asked, "What are the ingredients of happiness that deserve attention? Which ones do you want to intentionally cultivate and grow?"

Lilly, being the first person to join the conversation, emphasized the importance of practicing gratitude as a key ingredient.

Dr. Kathy then requested that they each share a way in which they have been cultivating gratitude.

Anna expressed her gratitude for her job and the financial stability it brings.

John expressed deep gratitude to God for Noah, who taught him the profound meaning of unconditional love.

Jake said, "My patients, their happiness brings me immense joy and fills me with gratitude."

Dr. Kathy assigned them a homework task. "Take the journal home and write down ten things you are grateful for in your lives. Then, make it a daily focus every morning."

Eleven

"The fool doth think he is wise, but the wise man knows himself to be a fool."

— William Shakespeare, As You Like It

The mornings started to change for John. He became more mindful and began living fully in the moment. He decided to break free from the usual rush to work. With a glance at his pending tasks, he would grab his coffee and settle by the window, observing the bustling crowd as they hurried to their jobs each morning.

As he approached his desk, he reached for his phone and found a message from Anna, "Need to talk. Can we meet after work, around 5:30?"

He replied, "Certainly, let's meet at the café located at the intersection of Wildwoods and Riles."

John got there first, took a seat, and promptly ordered two glasses of refreshing green juice from the waiter. As Anna walked in, John couldn't help but detect a subtle trace of unease etched upon her face. She joined at the table.

"Hey," she said, "answer me this: after all this time, you know me pretty well. Do you think I tend to be a bit paranoid, considering the amount of trauma and hardships I've faced? Do you think some paranoia can develop? I always remain hypervigilant, whether I'm walking through the busy streets or unlocking my front door after a shopping trip." Her voice faded as she spoke.

John smiled and reassured, "I don't believe there's much cause for concern. Remember when you used to meet Krishna in secret back home? It was a constant game of hiding and caution. Perhaps that same fear is resurfacing now."

"I'm sorry for being so emotional," she apologized.

John hugged her. "It's ok," he said warmly. "We can work through it together."

Anna nodded in agreement, and they both took a sip of their juices, relieved to have the conversation out of the way. However, as John looked into Anna's eyes, he could sense a lingering fear that wasn't easy for her to shake.

As they were preparing to leave, John invited Anna to their office party. "You should come," he said.

Anna responded, "Sure, but does that mean I'll officially become your girlfriend?"

John chuckled and replied, "Anna, my colleagues know you're in my life, but they're unsure if you're my friend or girlfriend. Whether we have a friendship or a romantic relationship, does it truly matter?"

After a moment of reflection, Anna replied, "Should we categorize human relationships? I think not. Once we assign labels, they become stagnant. They lose the potential for organic development and growth."

The office party was a splendid event. Anna wore an elegant, floor-length gown in a captivating shade of deep blue that beautifully highlighted her figure. Completing her ensemble, she adorned herself with a pair of earrings featuring blue sapphire and sparkling white stones.

John held her hand throughout the party. He couldn't stop looking at Anna. As the evening came to an end, they retired to his office for a nightcap.

"I had a great time," Anna said as she and John sat comfortably on the couch in his office. "Thank you for inviting me."

John's face lit up with joy. "I'm glad you enjoyed yourself," he said as he reached for her hand and intertwined his fingers with hers.

The two sat in comfortable silence, taking in the moment and feeling their connection grow even stronger. John then looked into Anna's eyes and asked, "Do you want to make it official?"

Anna smiled back at him and replied, "Yes, let's make it official!"

As they walked towards the car, Anna's happiness overflowed, causing her to tightly embrace John and shower him with kisses on his cheeks. However, an unsettling feeling started to creep over John. Acting on instinct, he abruptly turned around, catching a fleeting glimpse of a tall figure wearing a baseball cap, who quickly snapped a photograph.

John quickly dismissed the occurrence, but he couldn't help feeling unsafe. Was it his imagination? Or was someone trying to intrude on their special moment?

As they sat in the car, Anna excitedly recounted the numerous individuals she had encountered and the engaging conversations she had enjoyed with them. John, however, remained focused on the road ahead, his expression serious as he uttered, "Anna, do you remember mentioning that unsettling feeling of being watched? I believe there may be some validity to that. It might not solely stem from your fears or imagination."

John accompanied Anna to her apartment in a gated community. As a precautionary measure, he surveyed the area for safety. However, a sense of restlessness lingered within him. He politely requested Anna to enter and advised her, "Please remember to lock the door behind you and refrain from opening it during the late hours of the night. Feel free to reach out to me if you need anything at all."

Twelve

"No matter how much suffering you went through, you never wanted to let go of those memories."

— Haruki Murakami

It was a blissful federal holiday, and all Anna yearned for was a day of rest and rejuvenation. The previous week had been filled with non-stop work and commitments, and she longed to just put a brief pause on life.

Anna carefully selected her favorite scented candles and placed them strategically around the room. The soft, flickering light added an extra touch of warmth and coziness to her space. She then brewed a delightful cup of black tea, carefully infusing it with a blend of aromatic spices. The fragrant steam filled the room with a comforting and inviting aroma.

Taking a moment to pause and reflect, Anna wrapped her hands around the warm cup, feeling the soothing heat radiating through her fingers. She took a slow, deliberate sip, allowing the flavors to dance on her taste buds. The rich and bold notes of the tea brought a sense of comfort and relaxation as if each sip was a gentle embrace.

Just as she was lost in the moment, her phone broke the silence with a loud ring. It was Ma, calling from Home. The sound of her mother's voice always brought a smile to Anna's face. Although her father rarely made an appearance on the line. They would talk about everything from family updates to childhood memories, bridging the distance between them.

Recent news from home was filled with excitement and anticipation. Naina, Anna's younger sister, had recently completed her graduate program and was eagerly waiting for the perfect proposal.

"Naina received a wonderful proposal from a fine young man. They will be visiting next week. Naina and Dad are thrilled with the proposal," Ma said with excitement. In a hushed tone, Ma assured, "We won't discuss your divorce or anything of the sort. Instead, we'll simply explain that you are committed to work and, unfortunately, won't be able to attend the wedding."

"I understand, Mom," Anna said. "You know, if this proposal turns into a marriage, I can watch the wedding through a live stream if you all decide to do it that way."

Anna inquired about Dad's well-being. Ma replied. "He's quite occupied with making arrangements for the dowry and jewelry funds."

"Tell me about the boy, Ma," Anna asked.

"Well," said Ma, "the boy has a secure government job, and he is the only son. Their house is just 45 miles away. He has one married sister and no financial burdens. Moreover, they also own a farmhouse and livestock, so Naina will feel comfortable and at ease there."

"Ma, is Naina happy?" Anna asked.

"Naina is so happy, and the boy, he's quite handsome!" Ma said.

Anna smiled, imagining her sister's conjugal bliss. She knew Ma had done a great job finding the perfect match for Naina.

"I have to go now," Ma said. "We must make a bunch of snacks and everything for the girl meeting ceremony. I'm also planning to go to Parumala Church to say a prayer for the marriage to work out. I want this to happen. You know what happened to you. After your experience, we've decided that we'll never marry Naina off to a foreign country. Even Dad says she needs to marry into a good family in either our city or the next one. And she has to take care of us when we're old."

Anna remembered her own "meet the bride" ceremony, a dream that turned into a nightmare. In the kitchen, women adorned in vibrant silk sarees skillfully sliced an assortment of fresh vegetables. The aromas of fragrant spices filled the air, mingling with the laughter and chatter that echoed throughout the house. Meanwhile, the men gathered on the porch, engaged in lively conversations ranging from stories of their wedding ceremonies to the prices of spices.

Subsequently, an older female member of the family would gracefully guide the prospective bride to her slumber, ensuring there were no signs of fatigue or dark circles beneath her eyes. The bride was expected to radiate her innate beauty, exuding both vitality and a demure charm.

I hope everything goes well, thought Anna. Naina would be thrilled. She was the perfect match for the arranged marriage. Anna was about to go to bed, a little lost in her thoughts when John called.

"Hey there, how's everything going, darling?" he asked.

"Guess what?" Anna said. "Ma just told me that Naina might be getting married soon!"

"That's awesome," John remarked. "Are you going to the wedding, darling?"

Anna sighed softly. "Nope, they don't want me there! Divorce is such a taboo, and it's gonna affect Naina. But hey, it's okay, John."

"Anna, I'm sorry about that," John said.

"Well, I'll catch up with you soon," said Anna before she hung up the phone.

Thirteen

"In the end, these things matter most: How well did you love? How fully did you live? How deeply did you let go"?

— Gautama Buddha

Anna and John walked into the Saturday session together, immediately capturing Dr. Kathy's attention. She sensed a shift but decided to refrain from prying or discussing it. The rest of the group followed suit, silently agreeing to let the issue remain untouched.

Jake entered the room and went straight to the coffee table. "Oh, my goodness! I'm famished. This call was incredibly chaotic, keeping me awake all night," he said. "I'm feeling quite hungry as well. Once we're done, I must find a restaurant to satisfy my cravings, and then I plan on indulging in a full day of rest," he said, beaming.

Lilly entered with a radiant smile on her face. Her hair adorned with stylish new braids, adding a touch of charm to her overall appearance.

Anna complimented Lilly on her beautiful hairstyle.

" Jake, if you're up for it, I can take you to my all-time favorite Nigerian restaurant," said Lilly. "You know I grew up in Nigeria, right? Nigerian food is so satisfying, and that's what I'd totally recommend for you," Lilly chuckled. "We use palm oil for cooking, and believe me, it's like a magic sleep potion. After you have it, you'll sleep like a baby. That's my prescription for your post-call insomnia," Lilly continued. "It's heavy, but that's what I eat after a stressful day. It's my comfort food. We should go and try out different cuisines, and maybe we can add that to our Saturday schedule. After the session, let's all go out for dinner and try everyone's ethnic foods. It'll be a fun and delicious adventure!"

John loved the idea.

Jake remarked, "Anna, you'll be our guide to the flavors of Indian cuisine, while Lily will enlighten us with the delights of African dishes. And as for me, I'll treat you to the authentic taste of traditional Irish food, complete with shepherd's pie and a pint of good ol' beer."

"What about you, John?" Lilly asked.

John looked down and replied, "I wish I knew. I have no idea. Raised by foster parents, I am unaware of my biological parents or my ethnic background."

Just then, Dr. Kathy walked into the room. "That's one interesting conversation! What a great way to kickstart the day, right? We're all like our own little universe, and then there's this big, expansive universe that we all belong to. If we build walls, we're just limiting ourselves. Our lessons and growth start when we break down those walls so we can learn and evolve together. And guess what? When I put out the notice, I had no idea who would show up. But look at our group now, and it's like a whole expansive universe came together. Pretty cool, huh?"

"Alright, it's time to start the actual session," Dr. Kathy announced. "We'll begin with meditation and explore the realm of emotions and trauma that might hold us back on our journey. Let's work together to overcome these limitations and unlock our true potential."

She asked everyone to share a strong emotion tied to a past trauma that keeps coming back. "Once we figure out these negative emotions, they can be the key to unlocking our unconscious," she explained. "We must go there and clear out the mess, making space for positive thoughts, memories, and feelings to come in."

Anna expressed her feelings as "anger," while Jake admitted to having "no clue." Lilly, on the other hand, felt "betrayed," and John described his emotions as "helpless."

Dr. Kathy explained the importance of recognizing our emotions and identifying our triggers so we can move past them. She said, "When we understand that the same energy that created life also creates these feelings, we can start facing them head-on."

With a sense of purpose, she continued, "Here, take these as your key and dig deep. Close your eyes and picture yourself in that traumatic situation, with all those people who hurt you and made you feel this way". Then, she played some music, and everyone just closed their eyes and got lost in their thoughts.

Emotions ran high as tears filled the room, some evident, others hidden. Amidst it all, Jake remained silent and observant, taking in the array of feelings and reactions around him.

Dr. Kathy once again took the lead, highlighting the significance of embracing the reality of what occurred - a concept she called "Radical Acceptance." She then encouraged the group to recognize that, given the circumstances, everyone involved likely acted based on their understanding and perspectives.

Dr. Kathy stressed the importance of acknowledging the past to propel ourselves forward. Everyone acted and reacted based on their unique perspectives and life experiences at that specific time, which may differ greatly from what we now comprehend. It is intriguing to reflect on how much we have evolved since then, gaining new insights and knowledge along the way, she eloquently stated.

She then began a grounding meditation, inviting everything to settle - the trauma and the emotion. She revealed the secret: by visualizing these burdens, leaving without attachments or judgments, liberation awaited. Free from weight.

A palpable sense of relief permeated the room, spreading like gentle waves, embracing everyone except Jake.

Dr. Kathy's gaze shifted to Jake; her eyes filled with concern. "It seemed like you were somehow detached from all of this," she said.

"Yeah, I was," Jake replied. "I had an amazing life with perfect parents and a great education. I was bright, you know, and ended up getting into the best universities and medical schools. I didn't go through any of the traumatic experiences that my friends did. I guess I was just lucky."

"Jake, why on earth are you here?" Dr. Kathy asked, her voice filled with curiosity."

Jake replied with a hint of intrigue, "Perhaps it's time for my story."

Fourteen

"Let there be spaces in your togetherness and let the winds of the heavens dance between you. Love one another but make not a bond of love: Let it rather be a moving sea between the shores of your souls. Fill each other's cup but drink not from one cup. Give one another of your bread but eat not from the same loaf. Sing and dance together and be joyous, but let each one of you be alone, even as the strings of a lute are alone though they quiver with the same music. Give your hearts, but not into each other's keeping. For only the hand of Life can contain your hearts. And stand together, yet not too near together: For the pillars of the temple stand apart, And the oak tree and the cypress grow not in each other's shadow."

— Khalil Gibran, The Prophet

My home is in the beautiful countryside of Connecticut. My parents were well-off, upper middle class - hard working and loving. As a child, I was never exposed to any hardships that my friends here today endured. But I wasn't immune to life experiences either; in fact, I couldn't have been more different from them.

My parents were strict but fair, always encouraging me to reach for the stars. Our small yet close-knit family consisted of Dad, Mom, my brother, and yours truly.

Growing up, we had the privilege of attending a private school, where we received not only a top-notch education but also a protective and nurturing environment. It was a place where we felt safe to dream big and reach for the stars, knowing that we had a strong support system behind us every step of the way.

So, I was this kid who had everything going right. But there was a problem - a problem with me that wasn't too apparent in the beginning. I didn't have too many friends at school, you know? Like, I just couldn't make friends or keep them. I was a little odd there. No one thought much about it except for those occasional feelings of loneliness I felt. But I learned to cope. Just working hard and getting those great grades was my way of coping and making up for being partially socially handicapped.

The one thing that kept me going each day was music. Every morning, as soon as I woke up, I'd switch on the radio and listen to all kinds of music - from classical tunes to pop songs. Music is a universal language; it speaks in ways words can't express. Whenever I felt lost or alone, I'd just turn up the volume and find myself again. And oh! I forgot to mention the video games. So, my best friends were video games and music. My older brother used to call me a "weirdo" at times. I knew something was wrong with me, but I couldn't exactly define it, so I let it go and learned to live with it, you know, whatever shortcomings I had. I had these deep feelings but couldn't express them or connect with people. The only deep connection I was able to maintain was with my mother. I did some research and came to a self-diagnosis - Asperger's syndrome. While I can't be entirely certain, it seems to align with my experience as a highly functional individual with certain autistic traits.

.

It was in college when I hit a major roadblock. I wanted to have a girlfriend and be in a relationship. I thought my fancy cars would attract them, and they did, but they also left just as quickly. No one explained why, and to top it off, I got ghosted a few times, too. Before I knew it, it became a habit. There came a point where I wasn't even looking for relationships or love. I was just having a blast. So, girls came, and girls went.

It was during my cardiology residency when my mom introduced me to her friend's daughter. She was very pretty, tall, and a fine young woman. Her name was Maria. Maria was a quiet girl, and we started hanging out. Before we knew it, everyone was like, "Hey, you guys are a couple!" And just like that, we became a couple.

When I landed my first job, I mustered up the courage to propose to her, and to my delight, she said yes. It's complicated to explain, but we weren't exactly over the moon with excitement. But there was a special connection between us. I would say it wasn't quite the love in the traditional sense, but more like a deep sibling-like bond. I genuinely cared about her.

We got married, moved to Long Island, and bought our very first home. It was wonderful and had a huge garden and everything you'd want your home to look like. She loved gardening, so I chose this house to make her happy. I worked my butt off during that time, coming home late at night after long clinic hours. Even weekends were jam-packed. But Maria didn't complain, she didn't seem unhappy. I thought she understood I was busting my chops for both of us.

Fast forward one year, and I started noticing something. She was becoming quieter, and our conversations sort of dwindled, too. But I was working my tail off. I didn't have the time or the energy to notice any red flags. But soon, I realized that she felt lost and disconnected from me.

One day, I returned home from work, and an eerie silence engulfed me. The emptiness was palpable, casting a shadow over my soul. And then, I saw it - a solitary letter left behind just for me.

I unfolded the note, my eyes scanning the words that would change my life forever. "There is no point in continuing our marriage, Jake," she wrote. My heart sank, but her words held a truth I couldn't deny.

"I don't hate you," she continued, her concern evident in every stroke of the pen. "But something isn't right. You need to find a way to fix yourself for your own sake. Otherwise, you'll wander through life alone and disconnected."

Those words echoed in my mind, awakening a longing for self-improvement. It served as a wake-up call, prompting me to take self-discovery and personal improvement seriously.

. I didn't want to die alone like Maria said. The road ahead would be challenging, but I knew that by facing my demons head-on, I could create a life filled with love, connection, and true happiness.

I was hesitant to try traditional counseling because, as a physician, I didn't want my mental health care to go on record. So, I decided to explore something more spiritual instead. And that's how I ended up meeting Maya.

I was having a happy hour with my team - our monthly team-building session. Work can get super stressful, and we need to build a solid team, you know what I mean?

So, during one of these happy hours, I had the pleasure of meeting Maya for the first time. She happened to be a friend of my nurse, Elizz, and by chance, we were all at the same restaurant. Talk about serendipity, right? Anyway, Maya came up to Elizz, and Elizz casually introduced her to me. And let me tell you, I couldn't take my eyes off her. I mean, I'm not usually one to believe in love at first sight or anything like that, but it hit me like a ton of bricks. I was completely blown away.

I can't really explain it. She had this unique beauty, like something about her that just stood out. She was wearing this gown with a bohemian vibe, and her hair was so long, like, way past her hips. I couldn't tell where she was from or if she belonged to any specific place. It was like she was from another world. There was something so magical about her like she had stardust in her eyes. And her aura, her energy, it was just so captivating. I felt like I couldn't escape her presence and was totally stuck.

Honestly, for the rest of that happy hour, I wasn't even mentally there. I was physically present, but mentally, I was transported to another dimension.

The next day at work, I waited until Elizz was done with her tasks, and then I slowly approached her. I didn't wanna come off as desperate. So, I asked her if she wanted to grab a cup of coffee with me in the cafeteria downstairs so I could ask her about Maya.

Elizz had no idea, thank goodness! She's quite the talker, and with just a little coaxing, she spilled all the details. Turns out Maya runs this spiritual counseling center with a specialization in past life regression therapy. Elizz also revealed that she has undergone past life regressions herself.

I was naturally curious, so I asked Elizz if it helped her. And she was like, for sure! In past life regression therapy, the therapist guides you through hypnosis to explore your past lives. It's crazy, right? By experiencing these past lives, you can uncover things holding you back now. It's like tapping into your soul's memory or something. Like, if I have anger issues, I might be able to trace it back to a past life and learn from it to have a better life now.

I gotta admit, it all sounded kinda complex to me. But hey, Elizz was on board, too. I couldn't contain my excitement, so I just had to ask Elizz about Maya's background. Turns out Maya is biracial, with a Swedish dad and an Indian mom. But that's not all. She grew up in a vibrant cultural center in India, where her mom taught classical dancing.

After coming here to pursue her master's degree, she took an unexpected turn and became a past life regression therapist. Talk about an intriguing journey.

So, I asked Elizz the million-dollar question: "Is Maya single?"

Elizz replied, "Yeah, she is. You know, these spiritual beings aren't really into the whole typical relationships and stuff. They're more into their spiritual quests and all that."

I figured the way to Maya was to sign up for one of her past life regression therapies, so I asked Elizz if she could hook me up. Elizz didn't make any promises but said she'd ask Maya.

The anticipation built up inside me as the next day arrived. Every passing moment felt like an eternity, heightening my curiosity and excitement. Unable to contain myself any longer, I felt an overwhelming urge to ask Elizz if she had spoken to Maya. With each step toward my room, my heart pounded in anticipation.

As I reached my room, I caught a glimpse of Elizz through the slightly ajar door. She was completely engrossed in her work, her brow furrowed in concentration. It appears she was oblivious to my presence, lost in the world of her own thoughts.

Later, in the cafeteria, I anxiously scanned the crowd for any sign of her. Finally, I spotted her moving swiftly through the room, her mind seemingly occupied with her daily routine. Doubt started to creep in. Did she forget to ask Maya? Should I remind her about our conversation? A whirlwind of thoughts and emotions swirled in my mind, intensifying the sense of urgency that consumed me.

With each passing moment, the weight of uncertainty grew heavier. The need for answers became more pressing. Time seemed to slow down as I grappled with the unknown, yearning for resolution.

But then, a spark of light pierced through the darkness. Elizz abruptly stopped in her tracks and turned to me, her eyes aglow with excitement. "Maya specifically requested you to call her office and schedule an appointment. And guess what? It's with Tom."

As soon as those words left her lips, my world came crashing down. I couldn't help but ask Elizz, "Why Tom and not Maya? "

Elizz nodded empathetically and replied, "You know what, Jake, I wish I had an answer for that. Maya remembered you, but for some reason, she assigned Tom to guide you. Trust me, it's going to be a mind-blowing experience, and I'm sure you will have all the answers you need after your appointment with him."

I was so disappointed, like really let down. I was even angry! It was like life was starting to mess with me for absolutely no reason. Man, it was such a messed-up feeling. I was just tired of it all.

But then, Elizz said something that made me look at the situation in a different light. She said, Jake, sometimes we are handed an opportunity to explore our deepest emotions and regrets so that we can finally let go of them and learn how to heal ourselves from our past experiences."

It was then that I realized that perhaps I needed this journey and that Tom could help me understand why Maya sent me his way. All the anxiety and fear melted away, and suddenly, I felt a sense of determination to take on this challenge with open arms. But what made me decide was knowing that Maya would be there too in the office. At least I'd get to see her.

Finally, I mustered the courage to make that call, and to my delight, I secured an appointment for the following week. As the initial meeting commenced, it became clear that the focus was solely on unraveling the intricate tapestry of my life. Tom, with his attentive gaze, encouraged me to condense my life story into a nutshell. But it didn't stop there - he delved deeper, inquiring about the aspects of my existence I yearned to explore and understand.

He explained how the sessions would work. We might journey through time using hypnosis, exploring not only this lifetime but possibly other lifetimes. I couldn't help but wonder what secrets were hidden in my past lives, waiting to reveal the mysteries we had discovered. Maybe, just maybe, our focus would change and lead us to deep lessons and new knowledge that made us think. The anticipation was real.

Jake continued his story, saying, "From here on, things are gonna get a little weird, but hey, that's what makes it interesting, right?" He had this big smile on his face.

When I reached Tom's office, I was very nervous. I didn't quite know what to expect. Tom was very reassuring. He got a quick history of my present-day challenges, like a mental health synopsis, and then he explained the procedures to me. The next one was a little scary. He put me under deep hypnosis. Tom's hypnotic voice guided me into a profound state of relaxation. With each word, I descended into the depths of my being, transcending the boundaries of time and space. My eyes were closed, and I guess I was somewhere between the conscious and unconscious state of mind or something. I can't be sure! But here, I started to get visions. It was the 13th century or so, and I found myself living a past life in that era. I knew it was me. The best part is that you can remember most of this after you are back from hypnosis.

I found myself standing on a battlefield teeming with chaos, clashing swords, blood everywhere, broken bodies, and everything in between. Thank God this horror didn't last long. I was given a message at this point. I can't tell you where the message came from or who delivered it, but it felt like a download into my psyche. The horrors of war had compelled me to sever the cords of my emotions. I then chose a disconnected existence, free from deep emotions, a kind of emotional numbness and a lack of reaction or feeling, a sort of self-imposed exile in order to preserve my sanity to cope with the violence and war.

When Tom finally brought me back to conscious awareness, I was surprised at what I had found. The emotional disconnection and the innate inability to feel deep emotions were rooted in my past. Tom called it the DNA or cellular memory! I know there is no evidence-based medicine to support this one. But this was a very powerful revelation, and strange as it may seem, it made sense to me.

"So, what do you think?" asked Tom.

"I was impressed," I replied.

When I first heard about this, I wondered, "Is this some kind of black magic or what?"

Tom laughed out loud. "Do I look like someone who does black magic?"

He was wearing a white shirt, all neat and tucked into his sleek-black pants. His hair was closely cropped, and he wore this cool tie with stripes and a formal jacket. I mean, he looked like a total pro! And then he said, "I live just around the corner. My wife is a social worker, and we've got this 8-year-old boy who's in school. Just your typical American family." And man, he cracked up laughing!

That was when it hit me: he wasn't just some kind of guru. He was an ordinary guy who was good at helping people like me.

I must admit, my initial intention for attending the first session was simply to catch a glimpse of Maya. However, something changed within me as I continued attending more sessions. I found myself drawn to the experience for my own personal growth. During those sessions, I would occasionally catch sight of Maya. She would flash a smile before walking away, leaving me intrigued. Yet, it wasn't until that fateful day when our paths crossed at the local park that we finally had our first conversation.

So, it was a lovely spring evening, and I leisurely strolled through the scenic park in the heart of New York City.

So, there I was, sitting on this bench, just minding my own business. And guess who appeared in the distance? Maya, with her adorable dog, strolled along. She walked right up to me and plopped down next to me.

"Hey Jake, how's it going?" she asked.

"Oh, I'm loving it! I replied". "I've been having these great sessions with Tom, and I'm learning so much. Thanks for setting me up with him. I gotta admit, at first, I was kinda bummed that it wasn't you"."I paused for a second. "But hey, now things are cool."

Maya smiled. "I know."

Seeing her all relaxed and totally into this easy conversation, I couldn't help but be curious to know more. "Why did you reject me?" I asked. "I mean, I thought maybe you didn't have time or something."

She looked me straight in the eye. "You'll find out soon enough"." Then, she simply got up and walked away.

Man, talk about leaving me hanging! I couldn't help but wonder what she meant by that.

A few weeks later, I had another session with Tom. In the quiet room of Tom's therapy office, I settled into a comfortable recliner, ready to delve into the depths of my past lives. Tom began guiding me into a state of deep relaxation, preparing me for the journey that awaited. As I closed my eyes, I felt myself transported to the 19th century. I was standing in the picturesque countryside. The hills were adorned with a vibrant carpet of wildflowers. There was a cottage in the distance, and I saw some horse-drawn carriages pass me by on the cobblestone pathways. It was a feeling of pure bliss.

I started walking towards that cottage in the distance. I later realized that that cottage belonged to a local scholar, and he had a daughter - Keira. I instantly recognized Keira. She was Maya in her present life. This revelation was shocking to me. I instantly knew why I felt such an intense connection with Maya.

As Tom gently pulled me out of my deep trance, I was still in a state of shock and disbelief. I had encountered Maya, my soulmate. At that moment, everything became clear, including the unexplainable connection I felt towards Maya.

I anticipated that Tom might react with either disappointment or dismiss my revelation.

He didn't do either of those things. Instead, he simply nodded and transitioned to what I had discovered during my journey.

Intrigued by the mystery, I summoned my courage and posed the question to Tom, "What are your thoughts on the possibility of me having a connection to Maya in a past life?"

Tom remained silent for a while, leaving me in suspense, and then he responded, "You will come to discover what the truth has in store for you in due time."

With this newfound knowledge, my mind grew restless. I was consumed by the need to find her, to express myself, but deep down, I knew she understood. That's why she assigned Tom as my therapist. Determined, I requested an early morning session with Tom. After a few days, I finally sat in his office, urgency in my voice. "Tom, I have to talk to Maya. Just a few minutes, it's important."

Tom and I locked eyes, his gaze filled with unspoken thoughts. After what felt like an eternity, he finally spoke, his voice tinged with regret. "Jake, I'm sorry. Maya left yesterday. She's on her way to visit her parents, and I am not sure when she will come back?"

The uncertainty hung in the air, keeping us both deep in our thoughts.

I was shocked! Like, did she leave for good? But I didn't give up. I kept persisting and asked, "Tom, do you think you could give me her email or maybe some social media handle where I can reach out to her?"

Tom expressed, "Jake, I cannot divulge confidential information about my colleagues. It goes against the principle of confidentiality."

I understood the meaning behind Tom's words, and it hit me like a tidal wave. Devastation washed over me, leaving me speechless as I sat in his office. Sensing my despair, Tom kindly suggested going for a coffee. I reluctantly agreed, and we strolled down the street together until we stumbled upon a café. As we settled in, Tom took the initiative and ordered me a steaming cup of coffee. With a reassuring smile, he uttered those comforting words, "Let's maintain our focus and continue working on you."

I told Tom that I needed a break. I'll be back when I'm ready. But then I saw the notice about a small group where people gather to share stories, bond, and heal. It got me thinking about joining them. Tom was so supportive! He said, "Jake, that's a fantastic idea! It'll keep your learning process going, and you can always come back when you're ready."

As we exited the cafe, Tom turned to me and whispered, "Listen closely, my friend; fate has its way of reuniting souls. It's called divine timing. There's unfinished business between you and Maya. When the time is right, and you've learned the lessons you came to learn, you'll cross paths again."

I kept walking, lost in thought and curiosity. I discovered the reason for my emotional detachment and learned the art of feeling deeply. But alas, the object of my affection has once again vanished, leaving me longing for its presence.

What is the most important lesson I had to learn in this lifetime? I wondered. The pattern kept repeating, and I knew I had to break free from it. Love and loss, it's time to break this cycle. I yearned for a different experience this time around. Lost in my thoughts, I continued my journey, searching for answers. And then, it hit me like a revelation - I will keep feeling and loving, no matter what circumstances arise. I refused to become detached and stoic like in my past lives. They say love conquers all, and I won't allow loss or bitterness to consume me ever again. I'm committed to my journey of growth and learning, which is why I showed up at this meeting.

"That's an incredible story," John declared.

"Have you ever thought of writing about this?" Dr Kathy asked.

"No," Jake replied. "I don't know the end. I only know the beginning."

"Let's take a moment to reflect on everything we heard and learned today. So, shall we call it a day?" Dr. Kathy announced. "Yeah," everyone agreed.

Jake excitedly suggested going to an Irish cafe later that evening. "Today was a chapter of my story," exclaimed Jake. "Let's celebrate! It's on me."

Fifteen

"I would rather walk with a friend in the dark, than alone in the light."

— Helen Keller

Anna, John, Jake, and Lilly walked to the nearby Irish cafe. Nestled in the heart of the city, its exterior, adorned with vibrant flowers cascading from window boxes, welcomed visitors with a burst of color and warmth. The rustic charm of the cafe's stone walls, weathered by time, tells tales of generations past. Soft, golden light spills from the ceiling, casting a warm glow upon the worn wooden tables and chairs that invite patrons to linger and savor the moment. The walls are adorned with photographs and paintings, capturing the essence of Ireland's rich history and breathtaking landscapes. From the iconic Cliffs of Moher to the lively streets of Dublin, each image tells a story, transporting visitors to the heart and soul of the Emerald Isle. The sound of lively Irish music danced through the air and played softly in the background, creating a melodic backdrop to the conversations and laughter that filled the space. The clinking of glasses and the occasional burst of laughter create a symphony of joy, echoing the spirit of the Irish people.

Behind the counter, skilled baristas and chefs worked their magic, crafting steaming cups of Irish coffee and plates of hearty Irish stew. The tantalizing display of freshly baked soda bread, scones, and pastries beckoned with their golden crusts and mouthwatering aromas, laughter, and a sense of belonging. In this Irish cafe, time always seemed to slow down, allowing for moments of reflection and connection. It is a place where the spirit of Ireland comes alive, where the rich traditions, warm hospitality, and captivating beauty of the Emerald Isle are celebrated with every sip and every bite.

Anna, John, Jake, and Lilly sat around a small table, their faces beaming with excitement.

Anna took a sip of her Irish coffee and exclaimed, "I can't believe we're finally here, guys! So excited!"

"Hey, Anna! It's finally time for us to experience the luck of the Irish!" Jake chuckled.

"Shall we order the food?" John suggested and kindly asked the waiter to come.

The waiter placed the two plates of Irish soda bread on the table. "Here you go, folks. Enjoy! And what can I get for you?" He waited.

"Let's kick things off with four Irish whiskies and shepherd's pie!" Jake suggested.

The Irish whiskies were the first to arrive, and they joyfully raised a toast to their friendships. The smell of the Irish bread wafted through the air.

Anna, taking a bite, excitedly exclaimed, "This is like a piece of heaven on earth!"

"I'm curious: what makes Irish soda bread so special? Is it the ingredients or maybe the way it's baked?" Lilly asked with a smile.

"We always made it at home. Mom is an expert! Sometimes, I would watch her make it. Well, the secret lies in the combination of buttermilk and baking soda. It gives the bread its unique texture and flavor," Jake explained.

The Irish whiskey had cast its enchanting spell upon everyone as the music began to fill the air. An old Irish folk song echoed through the room, and with each chorus, the tables came alive with voices joining in harmonious unison.

In the emerald fields of Ireland, where legends come alive. There's a tale of love and courage that forever will survive. With fiddles and bodhráns, we'll sing this ancient song.

Of heroes and their battles, where righting wrongs belong.

Oh, raise your voices high, let the melody take flight.

In this Irish folk song, we'll dance through the night.

With a pint of Guinness in hand, we'll sing with all our might,

For the spirit of the Emerald Isle.

Shining ever bright.

On the rugged cliffs of Moher

where the waves crash with might.

A lass named Molly O'Connell

stood bravely in the fight.

With fiery red hair and eyes as green as the rolling hills.

She vowed to protect her homeland, with a heart that never stills.

Oh, raise your voices high, let the melody take flight.

In this Irish folk song, we'll dance through the night.

With a pint of Guinness in hand, we'll sing with all our might.

For the spirit of the Emerald Isle.

shining ever bright.

Through misty valleys and ancient ruins

our spirits intertwine,

With tales of banshees and leprechauns,

In every glass of wine.

From Dublin to Galway

the spirit's in the air

In this Irish folk song, we'll show the world we care.

And once again, they all joined the chorus, their voices intertwining in perfect harmony as they sang together.

Oh, raise your voices high, let the melody take flight.

In this Irish folk song, we'll dance through the night.

With a pint of Guinness in hand, we'll sing with all our might.

For the spirit of the Emerald Isle.

shining ever bright.

Once again, Jake exclaimed, "Here's to the company of great friends, the joy of delicious food, and the magic of unforgettable moments!" With glasses raised, they all took a sip, relishing the moment.

Anna was the first to break away from the enchanting music, her eyes sparkling with excitement as she leaned in to engage in conversation. "You know, one of the things I adore about our friendship is how wonderfully diverse we are. We come from different backgrounds, cultures, and experiences, yet there's this indescribable connection that unites us all. At the end of the day, we're all human, sharing this beautiful planet and chasing after the same dreams and desires."

John nodded in agreement and exclaimed, "If only the world shared this sentiment, we wouldn't be entangled in endless wars, and the world would be brimming with compassion instead of hatred!"

Lilly chimed in excitedly, "Absolutely! It's like having a miniature world right here at our table. We soak up so much knowledge and wisdom from one another."

Jake left everyone in awe with his profound revelation. "Fear is the invisible force that separates us. The fear of encountering souls adorned in different attire, treading unconventional paths, savoring exotic cuisines, or embracing divergent ideologies. We tremble at the sight of our superficial differences, perceiving them as imminent threats to our very existence. Our differences, however, are an opportunity encouraging us to step out of our comfort zones and embrace new perspectives."

Lilly wholeheartedly nodded in agreement, her eyes shining with enthusiasm. "Each of us brings something truly extraordinary to the table, and it's a beautiful tapestry that weaves magic into our lives in countless ways."

John concluded, "The change within us will create ripples, causing a transformative wave to ripple through the world. Positive vibrations have a way of spreading, just as negative vibrations do. So, in the end, perhaps we are lightworkers brought together to ignite a powerful, positive change. Who knows?" he said with a smile.

They all strolled out, their hearts filled with the magic of a beautiful evening. As they savored the moment, they pondered how things had transformed. What began as a gathering of four souls seeking some truths and gaining some insights had now taken on a life of its own, weaving a soulful tale.

Sixteen

"Out beyond ideas of wrong doing and right doing, there is a field. I'll meet you there."

— Rumi

Lilly was on a mission, determined to crack the code of saving money for college. She had exhausted all her options, yet her efforts fell short. Faced with an impasse, Lilly set her sights on an unconventional solution: becoming a paying guest.

Lilly began inquiring among her acquaintances if they knew anyone seeking a paying guest for their residence. Currently, she is paying $1500 for a modest apartment in Brooklyn.

It was a Saturday, and Lilly was working at Jake's office. Elizz was there, too, and during lunch, Lilly brought up this topic. She casually asked if anyone knew someone who might be interested in having her as a paying guest.

Elizz said, "Lilly, I'll introduce you to Adam and Harry. They're such a sweet couple. I've known them for ages. So, Adam wants to go back to school and pursue his passion for computer science, which means Harry is the one with the job now, working as a graphic designer at a local agency. They just need a little extra income until Adam finishes college and starts his career. I think you'll love them"!

Elizz shared their contact information with Lilly. Lilly made plans to meet up with Adam and Harry. I hope they like me, Lilly thought. I also hope they are open to getting to know a kind and genuine girl of African descent. You never know. She smiled.

When she arrived there, both Adam and Harry greeted her warmly and welcomed her inside. They showed her around the place before introducing themselves properly – they were both very friendly people who seemed genuinely excited about having Lilly live with them.

During the tour of the apartment, Lilly noticed how well-maintained everything was. It was obvious that these two men took pride in keeping things clean and tidy around here.

As if sensing Lilly's thoughts about this place being always so homey yet neat, Adam jokingly said, "It takes two men to make sure this place is spotless!" causing everyone to chuckle.

Adam escorted Lilly to her room, which had a private attached bathroom. A common living area awaited them, featuring two elegant white sofas and a dining table in an open kitchen, accompanied by two chairs. Harry couldn't help but exclaim, "Look, we'll have three chairs now!"

To Lilly's surprise, the rent was significantly lower than her initial expectations. Adam went on to explain, "As part of this arrangement, we believe in 'paying it forward.' When we first started out, we encountered countless obstacles. However, a kind stranger extended a helping hand to us. Now, we, too, wish to pay it forward."

As time passed, their initial casual acquaintance blossomed into a bond that felt more like family. Imagine older brothers looking out for their younger sister. But it didn't stop at just cleaning up; their collaboration went beyond chores. It started with shared dinners and movie nights, followed by animated conversations that frequently circled back to their university days. Their connection grew stronger as they discovered shared interests like music and nearby art exhibitions.

Before long, those small moments blossomed into regular occurrences, infusing each day with laughter and the thrill of shared adventures. Despite their diverse backgrounds and experiences, they found common ground in their love for late-night conversations, impromptu dance parties, and Sunday brunches filled with laughter and delicious food. In these simple yet magical moments, they discovered the true power of human connection, realizing that it transcends all barriers when we open our hearts, free from expectations and assumptions. Together, they proved that the bonds formed through genuine connections are the ones that shine the brightest, illuminating our lives with warmth, joy, and a sense of belonging.

Every morning, Lilly would light a candle before the statue of Mother Mary. Though she had known the pain of being motherless in her earthly life, she found comfort in the unwavering belief that her heavenly mother was watching over her.

As she gazed out at the Brooklyn Bridge, a gentle breeze caressed her face, carrying with it the scent of distant adventures and untold stories. The bridge became a symbol of connection, not just between the boroughs of New York but between her dreams and reality. It served as a reminder that anything is possible, encouraging her to take that leap of faith and chase after her aspirations.

And so, she sat by her bedroom window, night after night, inspired by the sight of the Brooklyn Bridge. It was a place where time stood still, dreams took flight, and where the magic of New York City came alive in all its grandeur.

And every evening, she wrote in her journal without fail, "I am a survivor. I am a divine creation of God. I am enough. I am love. I am enough. I am grateful for all my blessings. I am grateful for my job, and I am grateful for my friends Anna, John, Jake, Harry, and Adam. I forgive you, Pa and Oyibo; that's my gift to you, and I am letting go of my pain, and that is the gift I am giving myself."

Seventeen

"You yourself, as much as anybody in the entire universe, deserve your love and affection."

— Buddha

Jake eagerly dialed Tom's office, his anticipation palpable as he scheduled another transformative session. As Jake stepped into the room, he found Tom immersed in his thoughts, charting away. Catching sight of Jake, Tom exclaimed, "Glad you've decided to come back, Jake!"

A warm smile spread across Jake's face as he confidently declared, "I am now more invested in myself than ever before." Not a word was spoken about Maya. Without delay, they dived straight into the session.

After Jake left, Tom went straight to his computer and opened his email. He clicked on "New Mail" and typed in Maya888@gmail.com. Then, Tom scrolled down to the message section and wrote:

Dear Maya, I hope you've made it home safely. I can only imagine how amazing it must feel to be back, enjoying your mom's delicious home-cooked meals and having those heartwarming conversations with your dad by the waterfall you've always described. Oh, and by the way, how many masala chai cups have you already savored?

So, as promised, I wanted to give you an update on Jake. Guess what? He came back for a session! It seems like he's way more focused on himself now. And no worries, not a single word was mentioned about you.

Hey, keep me in the loop, alright? Sending my love to the whole family. Take good care, and until next time, bye!"

He signed off.

In the early morning, Maya gracefully rose from her slumber. Eager to embrace the day, she went into the bathroom and indulged in a refreshing cold shower. As droplets of water cascaded from her hair, she playfully tousled her locks. Adorned in a flowing white dress, she emerged, ready for the day.

Maya's parents ran a classical dance school and a center for yoga centered around prana breathing techniques. Many tourists and visitors would come and live in the guest house, taking classes. One of the main attractions of Varkala is its breathtaking beach, often referred to as Papanasam Beach. It is believed that a dip in the waters of Papanasam Beach can cleanse one's sins, hence the name "Papanasam," which means "destroyer of sins" in the local language.

Perched on the side of a cliff, Maya's home offered a breathtaking view. Just a stone's throw away from the house, a stream flowed with mineral-rich water.

Maya entered the kitchen and found her mother engrossed in preparing the fish. Arundhati, Maya's mother, embodied the grace of traditional beauty. Her name held the essence of elegance. With a dancer's physique and hair cascading in gentle waves down to her knees, she carried herself with an ethnic South Indian charm. Each morning, she would cleanse herself in the nearby stream, delicately wrapping a towel around her hair and elegantly securing it in a bun. After adorning her forehead with kalabham, a fragrant sandalwood paste obtained from the temple, she would then proceed to the kitchen to prepare lunch before commencing her dance classes.

"Mom! What kind of fish are you making today?" asked Maya excitedly as she sat on the kitchen floor.

"Meen Pollichathu, the dish you can't resist," Arundhati said with a smile. "Come and assist me. While I finish cleaning the fish, could you please prepare the masala, darling?"

Maya grabbed a spacious clay pot and poured in coconut oil. Next, she added two tablespoons of chili powder, one tablespoon of ginger-garlic paste, turmeric, coriander, fennel powder, and garam masala. She squeezed in lemon juice and used her bare hands to blend the ingredients into a smooth and flavorful paste.

Arundhati handed her the cleaned fish, and Maya finished marinating them and set them aside.

"Mom," Maya exclaimed, her voice brimming with anticipation, "there's something I have to share with you! I think I've found my one true soul mate!"

Arundhati sliced the green chilies and crushed the garlic together with fragrant curry leaves. She then turned to Maya and asked, "And where is he? You should have brought him along."

Maya was now frying the marinated fish in coconut oil. The oil was splattering and burning her skin a little. "I just mentioned that I've crossed paths with him. But he's not fully prepared for me just yet," she explained. "He's currently undergoing a profound learning process, healing his wounds and absorbing valuable life lessons. Only then can he truly align with me. We must have the same vibe when we merge spiritually. Ma is in a phase of his life called the dark night of the soul, and he is working through it now. He will be ready for me soon. I am waiting. I just know it.

You know why? Because we are connected by the invisible red string of fate"!

Arundhati got three large banana leaves and cut them into square pieces, large enough to wrap the fish. "So, when do we get to meet him?" Arundhati asked with a smile.

Maya carefully arranged the fried fish on the delicate banana leaves. With a generous hand, she spread the onion mixture infused with masala, creating a delectable layer of flavor. As she turned around, she expressed, "When he truly understands the concept of self-love, when he permits himself to experience profound emotions, and when he possesses the confidence to embrace vulnerability, only then will I meet him, and only then I can meet him." Maya smiled.

Arundhati folded the banana leaf over the fish, creating a neat parcel. She secured the edges with kitchen twine and started heating a pan over medium heat. She then turned over to Maya and, with an affectionate hug, said, "When I first met your dad in Dallas years ago, during a dance performance, I saw him and instantly knew he was my soulmate. It was as if time stood still. Without a word, he booked his tickets and followed me here. We exchanged vows at the local temple, and here we are!"

Arundhati placed the wrapped fish parcels on the pan and let it cook for about 5 minutes on each side until the fish was cooked through and the banana leaves imparted a smoky aroma.

"Mom, that's because you both were spiritually aligned at that point," Maya said.

Arundhati smiled and said, "Alright, we've finished cooking. What are your plans for the rest of the day?"

Maya stated, "First, I will attend Dad's Prana class. After that, I need to complete the remaining tasks for my book, respond to Tom, and then take a stroll along the beach."

Maya went to her room and switched on her computer. She read her rough draft of self-love. Then she started to type.

Why We Must Love Ourselves Before We Fall in Love

To experience a loving relationship, first and foremost, we must learn to love ourselves. Self-love is often misunderstood and overlooked in our society. We are taught to seek validation and love from others, to constantly compare ourselves to others, and to believe that our worth is determined by external factors. This mindset can be detrimental to our well-being and can hinder our ability to form healthy and meaningful relationships. When we don't love ourselves, we may find ourselves seeking love and validation from others in unhealthy ways. We may settle for less than we deserve, tolerate mistreatment, or become overly dependent on our partners for our happiness.

On the other hand, when we love ourselves, we can set healthy boundaries, make choices that align with our values, and prioritize our well-being. Self-love gives us a strong sense of self-worth and self-respect, which are essential for building healthy relationships. Loving ourselves also means accepting ourselves for who we are, flaws and all. It means embracing our strengths and weaknesses and understanding that we are worthy of love and happiness just as we are.

She saved the document and replied to Tom, saying:

Tom, thanks for the email. I hope you and your family are doing well. I've attached my initial draft summary of the book we discussed. Please look. I'm also sending you some pictures of my hometown. I hope you'll like them. Please keep me updated on Jake. Sending you lots of love, Maya.

Maya then rushed to join the Prana breathing class.

Eighteen

"All the world's a stage, and all the men and women merely players. They have their exits and their entrances; And one man in his time plays many parts."

-William Shakespeare

Lilly loved her new apartment, and she loved Adam and Harry. After a long day at work, she would return to a delicious dinner prepared by Adam and Harry. Each passing day brought a growing sense of belonging. However, some nights proved difficult. In the depths of sleep, she would be plagued by haunting nightmares and would wake up drenched in cold sweat. Lilly made a point to tightly shut the door. She didn't want Adam and Harry to hear her frightful screams in the night.

Jake's journey in therapy was a transformative experience, marked by profound shifts in his perspective and a newfound understanding of himself. Through countless sessions, he learned to feel the depths of his emotions, untangle the complexities of his inability to connect, and learn to embrace vulnerability.

Anna paced anxiously in her kitchen, her grip on the phone tightening as if it held the key to her heart. A deep longing to reconnect surged within her, bridging the vast distance that separated her from home. Her every fiber yearned to know the outcome of Naina's proposal, the anticipation building with each ticking second. Summoning every ounce of courage, she took a deep breath and dialed her mother's number. The phone rang, the suspense real as she held her breath and waited, hanging on the edge of her seat.

"Hey Anna, I wanted to give you a call and share some exciting news! Naina's marriage is fixed, and we are all super happy," Ma said.

"That is the best news I have received in ages," Anna replied.

"We're hoping that the groom's family remains unaware of your divorce. So, let's keep it under wraps, alright? You're not planning on attending, are you?" her mother inquired, curious to know.

With a heavy heart, Anna whispered, "Yes, Mom, I won't come. I promise".

Punished for sins that weren't mine, thought Anna. It felt unjust, but she realized the futility of resistance. Instead, she chose to embrace acceptance, recognizing that some battles are best fought by finding peace within.

John was focused on planning a romantic candlelight dinner to celebrate Anna's birthday. He wanted to make it an unforgettable day for Anna.

Finally, after much searching, John stumbled upon a lovely French cafe tucked away in the heart of downtown. He immediately knew it was meant to be - its old-world charm and pleasant ambiance served as a perfect backdrop for the evening.

He quickly booked the venue; he wanted it all to look picture-perfect for Anna's special day.

The night of her birthday arrived, and Anna was nothing short of amazed by the romantic setup - she had never seen anything so beautiful in her life.

Life unfolded with its natural ebb and flow, marked by the passage of days and nights, while the seasons transitioned, mirroring the ever-changing reality of their lives.

Nineteen

"One does not become enlightened by imagining figures of light, but by making the darkness conscious. The latter procedure, however, is disagreeable and therefore not popular."

— *Carl Jung*

Anna's anticipation for the Saturday session had been building all week. This gathering marked the final meeting for Dr. Kathy's current group and was dedicated to Lilly. In light of this, Anna took it upon herself to make it extra special. She spent the morning in the kitchen preparing some veggie patties for everyone to enjoy. She combined sauteed mashed boiled potatoes and peas with caramelized onions, rolling them into savory patties. While heating the oil to pan-fry the patties, her phone suddenly rang. She wiped her hands with a kitchen towel and answered. It was her mother on the line.

"Naina will be married in just two days," Ma exclaimed. "I'm really happy, Anna."

Anna, although genuinely happy for her sister Naina, felt a touch of sadness. She had hoped to be there in person to witness Naina's big day. Ma's next words didn't make her feel any better.

"You can watch the live stream on the YouTube channel," she added.

"No, Mom, I don't want to," said Anna in a low voice. "It will make me very sad."

There was an awkward silence, and Anna did not want to continue the conversation. "I have to go, Ma," she finally said and hung up the phone. Well, it is what it is, Anna thought to herself, refocusing her attention on frying the patties.

The doorbell rang, interrupting her cooking. Anna's face lit up as she opened the door and saw John standing there. He embraced her warmly before heading straight for the kitchen.

"Hmm, this smells delicious," John remarked as he took hold of a patty and began to eat it.

Anna attempted to smile, but John couldn't help but notice a lingering sadness in her expression. He had become so familiar with her that he could easily feel any hidden emotions.

"What is it, honey?" John asked gently.

Anna couldn't hold back her emotions any longer. "There's not much to say or add, and there's nothing I can do to change the situation. Naina is getting married in two days, and I am not welcome home. They are ashamed of me, John." Tears well in her eyes as she spoke.

John comforted her by putting his arm around her. "We will have a great time today," he assured her.

During the car ride to the session, Anna remained lost in her thoughts, the weight of her family situation heavy on her heart.

The last Saturday session was about to start. Jake entered the room, looking happier than ever. Lilly brought Harry and Adam along because it was her turn to share her story, and she wanted them to be there.

Dr. Kathy walked into the room; her face lit up with a smile. "It really seems like we've achieved what we set out to do," she began.

"Through these group sessions, the most significant outcome is that you've all rediscovered how to connect with yourselves. Without that self-connection, it's difficult to connect with others. At the end of the day, life is a beautiful symphony of connections and love we share. You all have awakened in a sense and will continue learning as you move forward. Meaningful connections have been made here. You may not have found a solution to every problem, but that's okay because problems change and evolve. The key takeaway is to be aware of who you are, connect with yourself, and value that connection."

Then, Lilly, with a mixture of apprehension and determination, announced, "Today is my turn to share my story, and I must admit, I don't think I can do it justice like the rest of you did, but I will try my best."

She took a deep breath and calmly sat down on the mat, her eyes moving between Harry and Adam. "I wanted them to be here, and now they will know the source of my nightmares."

The room fell into a hushed silence, filled with anticipation as Lilly prepared to share her story, a story that had been a heavy burden on her heart for a long time.

***

Lilly's Story

I grew up in a small village in Nigeria. We had one hospital, which was more like a medical center here, and two schools: a local school and a school for girls managed by a group of British nuns. My mother worked as a maid at a British school, while my father was an ambulance driver. We lived in a tight-knit community where all the families were connected. After I was born, my mother took me to Sister Rebecca, one of the nuns, who looked at me and said, "You must name her Lilly. She is so beautiful and radiant," and that was how I got my unusual name for a Nigerian.

My life was pretty ordinary, with nothing important to brag about. When I began school, Iye, that's what we call mother in Yoruba, enrolled me in a British school because she wanted me to receive a good education. Iye was loving and kind, even towards animals like stray dogs. I adored her.

Life took a tragic turn one morning. My mother contracted a severe and deadly strain of malaria, and before I knew it, she was gone. I was around 12 years old at the time. Iba, my father didn't even mourn Iye! He brought a woman home and announced that she would be my new mother. Everyone called her "Oyibo" because she had light skin and was beautiful. Since her arrival, Iba didn't even acknowledge my existence. Oyibo set the rules from day one. I was expected to come home, clean the house, wash the clothes, and prepare meals before I could even study.

Oyibo, my stepmother, became pregnant and gave birth to a beautiful baby girl. She was my half-sister, and I adored her with all my heart. Wherever I went, she would be right there with me, snugly wrapped up on my back, as I went about my daily chores.

But it was on one fateful day when I was just 14 years old and my baby sister was only two, that my worst nightmare began. As I struggled to lift a heavy bucket filled with scalding hot water...

***

Lilly's voice trailed off, and she couldn't hold back the flood of tears. She collapsed onto the mat, burying her face in her hands.

Sensing her distress, Jake approached and gently pulled her into a comforting embrace. "Hey, pumpkin," he whispered, "you don't have to keep going if you don't want to."

Lilly was determined. After taking a moment to compose herself and wipe away her tears, she expressed, "I want to confront and share my darkness. Have you heard of Carl Jung, the renowned psychologist? He believed in the power of facing our own shadow, bringing our deepest fears and hidden traumas to light. Do you know why? Because if we keep them locked up in our unconscious mind, they can haunt us throughout life. Sometimes, even insignificant triggers can unlock that door to darkness. These traumatic memories can overpower and cripple us. I need to release them. I don't want to be a prisoner of the darkness any longer. I refuse to be enslaved by my past. It's time for me to set myself free. I deserve happiness." Lilly paused briefly, then continued her story.

On that day, I was trying to carry hot water from the fire with my baby sister on my back. I thought I could handle it, but the pot was too heavy, and it fell. I got burned, but what concerned me more was that my baby sister's arm got scalded. Hearing her screams, Oyibo and Pa came running, grabbed her, and took her to the hospital. Thankfully, her injuries were minor. However, I ended up with major scars on my skin. While they eventually healed with time, the emotional scars from that day have never truly healed. They linger like an open wound, emitting a darkness that I constantly try to keep locked away.

After they returned from the hospital, the whole family gathered to determine the punishment I deserved to prevent a repeat of my actions. They settled on 20 lashes with a leather whip. I was instructed to undress to my undergarments, and the eldest member of the family tied me to a tree and administered the lashes. The rest of the family watched as I initially screamed in pain, but I eventually felt a numbing sensation. I dissociated and couldn't remember much. Perhaps I lost consciousness.

When I woke up at night, I put my clothes back on and attempted to walk, but the pain was unbearable. Taking slow, painful steps, I made my way into the woods. There was a tree there, under which I used to sit and talk to my Iye. I sat under that tree and cried, pouring out my heart. I pleaded with Iye to take me with her. Exhausted, I lay there under the tree and drifted off to sleep. That night, I had a dream. Iye appeared and cradled my head in her lap, showering me with love. She looked into my eyes and said, "I can see what you can't see. I can see far into the future. You have an incredible life ahead of you. Babe, just keep moving forward. I am by your side. Leave home and go to Sister Rebecca; she will take care of you. Never return home. I am always with you."

***

Lilly paused for a minute as if catching her breath, and then she rolled up her sleeve. "That night, I was stripped of my modesty and dignity and was publicly humiliated and traumatized. But look here," she showed the tattoo on her arm. In bold letters, there was an inscription that read, "I am a survivor."

"When I first joined this group, I felt lonely and struggled to make friends. I wasn't sure if I would be accepted. Loneliness can be like a disease, you know? I lacked the confidence to initiate conversations with anyone." Lilly's voice wavered for a moment, but she pressed on. "I wanted to break down my walls and let go of some of my burden and inner darkness, not all of it, but some." She smiled and looked around. "Now, I am grateful. I have found my tribe."

The group fell into a hushed silence. Dr. Kathy guided Lilly to an adjacent room and whispered, "I have the contact information for one of my friends, a trauma specialist therapist. Give her a call."

When Lilly returned to the room, Anna began distributing the patties she had prepared. Jake collected everyone's contact information to ensure they could stay connected. A bittersweet feeling washed over everyone as the group sessions came to an end.

As Jake was leaving, he approached Lilly and gently placed his arm around her. "You can count on me. I'll always be there for you, like family."

Lilly nodded. "Thank you, Jake."

Adam and Harry were speechless. They wiped away their tears, unable to find the right words to say. Harry held onto Lilly tightly, unable to speak. Finally, Adam found the courage to speak up.

"Lilly, we're family now. You'll never be alone. We'll always love you, no matter what. We're here for you, and you're here for us," Adam said, his voice filled with emotion.

Lilly looked at Adam and Harry, tears still streaming down her face. She felt a mix of sadness and hope. She had never experienced the love of a family before, but in that moment, she felt a glimmer of something she had always longed for.

"Thank you... thank you both so much," Lilly whispered, her voice trembling. She held onto Harry's hand tightly, feeling a sense of belonging she had never known.

In the depths of her thoughts, Lilly pondered the age-old adage, "Blood is thicker than water." Yet, she couldn't help but question its validity. Sometimes, the very blood that courses through our veins can be tainted with poison and toxicity, while the water, like our chosen family destined or given to us as a gift, becomes our saving grace, liberating us from the currents of poisoned blood.

Lilly left with Adam and Harry.

John and Anna left together in his car.

Twenty

"Named must your fear be before banish it you can."

— Yoda

It was the weekend, and Jake attended his last session with Tom. Tom motioned for Jake to sit across from him and presented a folder. "Here's the summary of our therapy, key takeaways, and some exercises for cognitive restructuring."

Jake accepted the folder and began to peruse its contents. "I'm amazed at how much ground we've covered," he remarked.

Tom leaned back in his chair, a mischievous grin playing on his lips. "And I have some exciting news for you," he said. "Here's' Maya's number. She wants you to give her a call. She just completed her book on self-love and is now working on a project about yoga. She could use your expertise in medical literature."

Jake's heart swelled with overwhelming joy. All that managed to escape his lips was a heartfelt expression of gratitude. "Thank you, Tom."

Tom chuckled. "Thank you for the therapy or phone number?" he teased.

"For both," he replied with a laugh.

On the drive home, Jake cranked up the music and sang along, feeling truly alive in that moment. It had been a while since he had experienced such happiness.

When he arrived back home, he immediately dialed his mother's number. The joy in his voice was so palpable that his mother couldn't help but feel a bit puzzled. She proceeded to fill Jake in on the preparations for the upcoming family reunion, urging him to mark the date on his calendar.

Lost in his own thoughts, Jake absentmindedly asked his mother, "So, what's happening, Ma?"

Taken aback, his mother replied, "I just informed you about our family reunion. Please don't tell me you didn't hear anything. Are you alright?"

"Mom, I believe I've fallen in love," Jake blurted out.

"Who is the girl?" she asked. "You've never mentioned anyone before, Jake."

"I understand, I understand. What I mean to say is that I have found my soulmate, and her name is Maya. I intend to reach out to her soon," Jake explained.

His mother, while bemused, couldn't help but chuckle. "I have never heard anything quite like this from you before. You claim to have met a girl whom you are convinced is your soulmate. However, you have not yet spent time with her or engaged in any meaningful conversations, yet you believe yourself to be in love. Is that a correct summary, Jake?"

"Mum, I'm really sure about Maya. The only problem is I can't fully explain why. If I try, you might think I'm crazy," Jake said with a smile.

His mother chuckled and replied, "I always thought you were a bit different, not like everyone else. A lateral thinker, you go off the tangent, not mainstream".

"Yes, Mother, you've got it spot on. I understand, and I truly understand. And there are these moments... I mean, when it's a connection beyond explanation, you simply know, Mom," Jake replied, once again immersed in the realm of dreams.

Jake asked, "Okay, do you want me to explain?"

His mother reassured him, "Please don't worry about being judged. Tell me."

"Mom, Maya has these beautiful brown eyes, like hazelnuts! That's the first thing I noticed about her. When I look into her eyes, it's like I can see her soul. It feels so familiar, like we've known each other for a long time."

"That's the first time I've heard you say something like that, Jake," Mom said, still not convinced.

"Trust me, Mom, please," Jake reassured her.

"You always talk about Lilly, your new adopted sister. Why don't you bring her over, Jake?" Mom extended an invitation.

"Sure, Mom, I Love you. Catch up later," and Jake hung up.

Mom wanted to hear more about Maya but from Lilly's perspective.

The next day, Jake arrived at work and eagerly awaited Lilly's arrival. She was the second person he wanted to share the news with.

As Lilly entered the office, Jake approached her with a smile on his face. "Are you okay, pumpkin?" he asked, affectionately wrapping his arms around her.

"Yes, I'm fine," she assured Jake. "I'm about to begin trauma therapy."

"That's great to hear," he said.

As they pulled away from the embrace, Jake couldn't wait to share the news with her. "Alright, I have Maya's number, and I'll be giving her a call soon," he beamed.

"That's wonderful, Jake! But take your time, and don't be hasty," Lilly cautioned.

"I will, Lilly. Thanks," he said, giving her shoulder a gentle squeeze before hurrying off to the cath lab.

Lilly went to her table and began working. Suddenly, her phone rang, and she glanced at the screen to see Anna's name displayed.

"Lilly, can I have a minute?" Anna's voice came through the phone.

"Of course," Lilly replied, sensing a hint of sadness in her voice.

"Can we meet at the coffee house this evening?" Anna asked. "I need to talk, and if you're available, it would be great to catch up."

"Sure," Lilly replied before ending the call.

As the clock ticked past 6 p.m., Lilly made her way to the nearby Starbucks. When she entered, her eyes quickly located Anna sitting near the corner window, looking elegant in a light blue dress with puffed sleeves. They exchanged greetings, and both ordered tall cappuccinos.

Breaking the silence that had settled between them, Anna began, "Lilly, you're aware of John and me, aren't you?" She paused, awaiting a response.

Lilly smiled. "Well, we've all been aware of it, eagerly waiting for the moment when both of you would reveal your love story."

"I hope it stays as a love story, girl," Anna said softly.

Lilly leaned in, her concern evident. "What's the problem in paradise?"

Anna hesitated for a moment, her gaze fixed on her coffee cup. "It's not John, it's me."

"Just say it, hun," Lilly urged.

Anna took a deep breath, gathering her thoughts. "A few things happened. My sister, Naina, got married, but I wasn't allowed to attend. My parents expressed their shame over my divorce and asked me to stay away. Later, my mother called to describe how beautiful the wedding was, despite previously telling me not to come. I claimed to be busy and abruptly ended the conversation. This whole situation triggered a flood of memories, emotions, and self-doubt. Unfortunately, these dark emotions started to affect my relationship with John. And now, I find myself questioning: Did we rush into this commitment too hastily? Is what we have real love or Limerence?"

"Limerance? What on earth is that, Anna?" Lilly asked, her face filled with confusion.

"Limerance is similar to infatuation. You fall into it quickly, experience a rapid crescendo, and then it diminishes as quickly as it began," Anna explained.

"Okay, I understand. Love and infatuation are two complex topics for me. What I do know is that this overthinking and constant analysis is like a curse in our modern society. Instead of allowing something good to naturally evolve between people, we tend to analyze and overthink it, ultimately ending it prematurely. If it's something good, why not let it grow naturally while enjoying the process? Why do we feel the need to dissect and overanalyze it, ultimately killing it? Lilly asked.

Anna paused for a moment and replied, "I guess it's like that saying, once bitten, twice shy, you know?"

"So, where's John, Anna?"

"On a business tour, won't be back until the end of June."

"Does he keep in touch?"

"Every single day! Each morning, he sends me a sweet text filled with love, and by the end of the day, he calls to share every little detail of his day with me," Anna said, a smile lighting up her face.

"Okay, Anna, you don't have to worry," Lilly reassured her.

Changing the subject, Anna asked, "How is Jake doing?"

Lilly chuckled, lightening up. "The boy is absolutely smitten, head over heels in love with Maya, even though he hasn't even spoken to her yet. Funny enough," Lilly burst into laughter, "that's what I truly admire about Jake. He doesn't overanalyze things. He dives in with all his heart, and maybe, just maybe, he's got it right while the rest of us misread the situation."

"Have you ever been in love, Lilly? Anna asked.

Lilly couldn't contain her laughter as she began to share her unique love story. "I have this one love, or at least that's what I call it - my chocolate milk love story," she chuckled. "It all started with a boy who lived next door; his name was Romance. We were probably in middle school, I think. There was this old man we all called Aburo, who would come around once a week and give us ice-cold chocolate milk. Let me tell you, it tasted even better than the most delicious candy back in those days. We would each get just one cup, and I would always drink mine in one big gulp, always wanting more. But Romance, he had a special fondness for me. He would share his chocolate milk with me as if it was our little secret. It went on until I had to leave and live with Sr Rebecca. That's about it."

"Now I feel like having ice-cold chocolate milk," Anna smiled.

"It's getting late, dear. We have to go next time," Lilly said.

Lost in her thoughts, Anna awaited the arrival of the cab driver. "It's the hidden fear within me, stemming from past trauma, that is now intertwined with my love for John," she pondered. "I must confront this fear before it erodes all that is precious to me at present."

Twenty-One

"I am grateful that you were born, that your love is mine, and our two lives are woven and welded together."

— Mark Twain.

Jake glanced at his watch, his anticipation growing with each passing second. The morning coffee sat untouched, forgotten in his excitement. With a sense of joy and eagerness, he carefully inscribed "June 1, 2023" into his journal, a date that held significance for him. Finally, he dialed Maya's number, his heart pounding in his chest.

As Maya appeared on the FaceTime screen, Jake found himself momentarily speechless. She wore a white Kurtha and a flowing skirt, her long tresses dancing freely around her. Seated amidst the serenity of her garden, she exuded a radiant glow that captivated Jake completely.

Maya greeted him with a warm smile. "Hello, Jake."

A nervous smile played on Jake's lips as he struggled to find the right words. "Gosh, you look so beautiful!"

Maya's laughter filled the air, her amusement evident. "Thanks anyway. Do you say this to every woman you meet for the first time?"

Jake joined in her laughter, his nerves easing. "Not...not really," he stammered, "I have no idea what came over me."

"Jake, are you a flirt?" Maya asked. "If you are, you're not a bad one."

Jake quickly interjected. "I am not a flirt, to be honest. I often find myself saying the wrong things to women."

Shifting gears, she brought up the topic of the book. "So, about the book Tom mentioned. I'm writing a book on yoga, and I would love for you to help me write a synopsis focusing on the cardiovascular benefits of yoga. Can you do that?"

"Sure, I can. When do you need it?"

"Take your time, Jake. There's no rush."

Filled with curiosity, Jake couldn't help but marvel at Maya's surroundings. "Maya, it looks like you're in some tropical paradise," he remarked.

Maya smiled. "Do you want to see around? I can show you." Without waiting for his answer, she began to give him a virtual tour of her home.

As Maya moved through the house, Jake's eyes widened with wonder. She pointed out the entryway, with a sprawling garden that served as a serene backdrop for meditation classes. Her mother, it seemed, taught dance lessons in the open veranda. Maya guided him further, revealing a long hall that led to the kitchen.

Seeing the kitchen, Jake exclaimed, "There's a lot of cooking going on in there, isn't there?"

"That's for the big lunch we're having today for the meditation group." Realizing that time was passing, Maya gently added, "I guess I'll have to let you go now. You've got to rush to work, right?"

Jake, feeling no rush and enjoying their conversation, glanced at his watch and replied, "I'm not in a hurry."

"I have to go now, Jake. Call me when you have the synopsis ready, okay?" Maya bid him farewell and hung up the phone.

As the screen went dark, Jake was left with a profound sense of bliss and excitement. It was a feeling he hadn't experienced in a very long time.

Maya was walking along the sandy shore, the beach just a stone's throw away from home when Jake's message popped up on Maya's screen. Hey, sweetie, I have your synopsis ready. Can we indulge in a FaceTime rendezvous soon?

Reading his words, a smile graced her lips. "Hey, sweetie," she mused, "This man possesses a gift for eloquence and a charm that flows effortlessly." She typed back, We can now.

Almost immediately, Maya's phone rang.

"I have taken great care to create everything exactly as you desire, sweetie," Jake said.

"Sweetie? Jake, do you use such poetic language with every woman you meet?"

Caught off guard, Jake chuckled and confessed, "Not with everyone."

"So, you address me as sweetie, but what am I to call you in return?"

"Feel free to shower me with any endearing term you wish, my love," Jake replied.

Maya's laughter resonated like a symphony, filling the room with joy as she playfully bantered, "Ah, once again, you've managed to add an extra layer of enchantment. Now, it has transformed into love. I guess I will have to adapt to this new reality, Jake. Very well, send me the synopsis, please."

Without delay, Jake dispatched a text accompanied by an attachment.

Maya's curiosity remained unabated, and she inquired, "This is quite impressive. Did you truly pen this yourself? Did you painstakingly gather all the research material?"

Jake couldn't bring himself to lie to her. He lowered his gaze and said, "No, my dear. I had the help of my research assistant in creating it. I wanted to have it ready for you before I leave for the upcoming conference."

Maya continued to wear her smile and responded, "That is perfectly acceptable. Please extend my gratitude to your assistant. Should I require further additions or have any inquiries, I shall reach out to your assistant"?

"Hey, don't worry. I'll only be gone for a few days, and we'll work together on this project," Jake said. "You can't get rid of me that easily."

"I have no intention of parting ways with you, and even if I desired to, it would prove an impossible feat."

Suddenly, Jake's demeanor changed. "Why did you say that?"

Maya swiftly averted her gaze, diverting the conversation. "Do you want to see the beauty of our local beaches and cliffs? They have a captivating beauty that is truly unique when illuminated by the evening's twilight touch." She turned the camera, showing the breathtaking sight of the sun's descent and the waves crashing against the cliff, shattering into a myriad of glistening droplets.

Maya turned the camera back to face her. "Did you enjoy your tour of our local beach? she asked, smiling. However, her amusement quickly faded as she noticed that Jake looked serious.

"You didn't answer me; why did you say you have no intention of parting ways with me even if you desired to?" he asked again.

Maya hesitated for a moment before responding. "You already know the answer to that. But I don't want to discuss it right now." Trying to lighten the mood, she smiled again and said, "On the bright side, I'm having fun with this flirtatious banter and our book discussion."

Jake continued to gaze at her, the silence between them growing increasingly awkward.

Sensing the need to change the subject, Maya quickly shifted the conversation back to the book. "Jake, do you happen to know anything about yoga?"

Jake's serious expression softened. "I do," he replied. "I've dabbled in yoga for a while now. By the way, how's the rest of the book coming along?"

Maya was relieved that the subject had changed again. "It's coming along well. I've been researching and gathering information on different aspects of yoga, and it's been quite an enlightening journey. I'm passionate about spreading awareness of the benefits of yoga to a wider audience."

"That's amazing, Maya!" Jake said. "I admire your dedication and passion towards this project. I truly believe that yoga has numerous benefits, not just physically but also mentally and spiritually. It's great that you're shedding light on the cardiovascular benefits specifically".

"Yoga is a holistic practice that can benefit our overall well-being. The cardiovascular benefits are often overlooked, but they are significant. I want to highlight how yoga can improve heart health and contribute to a healthier lifestyle," Maya replied.

As the evening wore on, Maya reluctantly stood up from her spot, realizing that her parents would start to worry if she stayed out any longer. "It's getting late, Jake. I should head home," she said.

Jake's face fell slightly, but he understood the need for her to leave. "Is your home near this beach, Maya?" he asked.

"Barely a 5-minute walk. It's conveniently close."

"Alright then, I'll talk to you soon. Go over the draft I sent you, sweetie."

"Ah, there you go again," she laughed, enjoying their banter.

"I'll call you tomorrow. Nighty night, love," Jake said.

"You're such a flirt," Maya responded. "And 'nighty night,' that's the first one I haven't heard in ages."

With a final exchange of laughter and playful words, Maya ended the call and began her journey home.

As Maya walked home, the cool evening breeze brushed against her face, carrying with it a sense of contentment. She couldn't help but replay the conversation with Jake in her mind, feeling a growing connection between them. The way he called her "sweetie" and "love" made her heart flutter, and she found herself eagerly anticipating their next conversation.

Arriving at her doorstep, Maya entered her home to find her parents waiting anxiously.

"Maya, where have you been? We were worried sick!" her mother yelled.

"I'm sorry, Mom. I lost track of time."

Her father's stern expression softened as he hugged her tightly. "Just remember to inform us next time, Maya. We care about your safety."

Maya nodded, feeling a mix of guilt and gratitude for her parents' concern. She retreated to her room, eager to review the draft Jake had sent her. She turned on her laptop, clicked to open the document, and started reading. As she delved into the synopsis, her mind wandered back to her conversation with Jake. She loved his playful nature and the way he effortlessly charmed her. A profound sense of gratitude washed over her for the serendipitous connection she had found with Jake.

The next morning, Maya's eyes fluttered open as the first rays of sunlight streamed through her window. Looking at the clock, she realized it was already 6 a.m. It would be around 6 p.m. in New York, where Jake was, and he might be getting ready to board his flight for the conference. Maya decided not to call him. He could be rushing to the airport, and she didn't want to disturb him. Instead, she opted to go for a morning stroll before breakfast.

As she walked along the serene path, the cool breeze gently caressed her face, clearing her mind. Maya took the opportunity to reflect on her own goals and aspirations. She mentally compiled a list of the tasks she had set out to accomplish for herself.

Upon returning from her stroll, Maya found two missed calls and a text from Jake. The text read: Got worried when I didn't hear from you. Just wanted to let you know I am boarding now. Talk to you soon.

A smile spread across Maya's face as she read Jake's message. She texted back, Safe travels. Will talk to you soon.

Maya, halfway across the world, was still in a deep sleep when Jake sent her pictures. The following morning, she groggily glanced at her phone and noticed the unread messages. A smile formed on her lips as she looked at the pictures he had sent. She quickly composed a response. Nice pics.

Almost immediately, Jake came online and replied, that's all you gave me, babe?

Maya chuckled at his response and texted back, "Okay, you're cute."

"Cute, that's all I get, love? Am I that bad?"

Maya sensed his vulnerability and decided that it was time for a real conversation. Call now. I prefer talking to texting.

Moments later, Maya's phone rang, and she answered. As their conversation continued, Maya took a moment to look at Jake. He was wearing a crisp white shirt with a few buttons undone, revealing a glimpse of his chest, paired with stone-washed jeans. Maya was overwhelmed by his good looks.

"Okay, you're good-looking, handsome," she finally managed to say.

"That's better, love!"

They continued their conversation, discussing various topics, including the synopsis that Jake had sent Maya. She expressed her appreciation for it but also mentioned that she would need citations and references plugged in. Jake assured her that he would take care of it. After a brief goodbye, Maya concluded the call and hurried to the kitchen to set the table for breakfast.

Twenty-Two

"If I had a flower for every time I thought of you, I could walk through my garden forever."

— Alfred Tennyson

Days turned into weeks, and before they knew it, almost a month had passed since Jake and Maya began their long-distance conversations. During this time, Maya had successfully completed her book and sent it off for publication. However, amidst the excitement of their growing connection, both Jake and Maya seemed to forget about the book as their daily conversations took precedence.

Every morning, as the sun rose, Jake would sip his coffee and dial Maya's number. As soon as she answered, he would greet her with a warm "Morning, love" before delving into the details of his plans for the day. Their daily morning calls had become a routine, a way for them to start their days together despite the physical distance between them.

In the evenings, Maya would sit on a rock overlooking the serene beauty of her surroundings. It had become their designated spot for their evening chats, a place where they could unwind and share the events of their day. Maya would vividly describe the dishes she had cooked, introducing Jake to the flavors and aromas of Kerala cuisine. Through her words, he could almost taste the spices and feel the warmth of her kitchen.

By the time July arrived, the monsoons had made their grand entrance in Kerala. Maya eagerly awaited Jake's call, excited to share the experience of the pouring rain with him. She sat on the rock as the raindrops fell with a vengeance, drenching her completely. Her white dress clung to her like a second skin, accentuating her beauty amidst the downpour.

The phone rang, and Maya's heart fluttered with excitement. "You have to see and experience the monsoons, Jake," she exclaimed, turning the camera towards the downpour. She wanted him to soak in the magic of the rain and feel it through the screen.

With a gentle turn, Maya redirected the camera towards herself, settling on an old wooden bench in the fisherman's cabin. As Jake's gaze met hers, an intense desire surged within him, coloring his cheeks with a rosy hue. He struggled to conceal the depth of his longing, unable to find the right words to express the passion that had awakened within him. Finally, he managed to utter, "You are absolutely gorgeous!"

Maya chuckled and responded, "I've heard that before." But as she looked into Jake's eyes, she couldn't ignore the desire that flickered within them. "Why are you looking at me like that?" she asked.

"Because I love what I am looking at now," Jake replied.

"And what exactly are you loving about what you see?"

Without hesitation, Jake confessed, "All of you."

"Do you want to see more?" Maya asked.

A resounding "yes" escaped Jake's lips, his curiosity and desire intertwining.

Maya entered the cabin and carefully placed her phone on an old chair. The cabin had been abandoned for years, its emptiness adding an air of mystery. She lowered herself to the floor, her fingers deftly undoing the buttons of her white dress, revealing the vulnerability beneath. Her hair cascaded over her bare breasts, a delicate veil of modesty. Slowly, she turned, a sensual smile playing on her lips as she parted her hair, exposing her supple, soft curves to Jake's gaze.

Overwhelmed by her beauty, Jake found himself repeating, "You're so incredibly beautiful, my love." The words spilled from his lips, overflowing with love for her. "God, I love you so much," he confessed, his longing to hold her and kiss her growing with each passing moment.

Maya's laughter filled the cabin. Then she playfully declared, "Enough for now," and she slipped the dress back on. With a smile that held promises of future encounters, she bid him farewell. "We'll talk later. I need to hurry home."

Jake smiled, the memory of Maya's beauty and their shared desire lingering in his mind.

The next morning, Maya woke up to the sound of the phone ringing. It was Jake. Still half-asleep, she groggily answered the call, her voice tinged with drowsiness.

"Babe, is it still raining there?" Jake asked. "I adore your monsoon rains!"

Maya chuckled as she revealed the clear blue skies above. "You know, Jake, monsoons have a profound effect on me."

"That's fantastic. I'm still amazed by what it did to both of us."

"I'm not joking, Jake. The monsoons awaken something deep within me. It's difficult to put into words, but it's like a sensual awakening. Every time it rains, I feel an intense connection to my feminine energy, and that's what you witnessed."

"I hope it rains every day," Jake playfully remarked.

"Okay, now I have to ask you something serious."

Jake leaned back, ready to listen and respond. "Go ahead."

"You said something yesterday. You said you love me. What was that about?"

Jake was unfazed by her question. "Why does it surprise you, Maya? I've always made that very clear from the first time I met you. It was you who ran away."

Maya averted her eyes, searching for the right words. "I know, but you weren't prepared for me."

Confusion etched across Jake's face as he sought clarification. "Prepared? Can you explain that?"

"We were on different spiritual levels, Jake," Maya said. "At that time, I was more evolved than you. You needed to delve within yourself and find your own path because I exist within you. Until you can explore your inner depths, you won't be able to discover the me in you."

Jake looked at Maya, a newfound understanding dawning in his eyes. "I get that now."

"After that, you must have dated other women, right?" Maya asked, her smile hinting at playful curiosity.

Jake's expression turned serious. "No, no one. Something changed within me after I met you. I lost interest in casual dating. I needed to understand why that happened, which is why I agreed to undergo past life regression therapy."

"And did that past life regression therapy help you?" Maya asked.

"It did," Jake replied. "I was able to gain a better understanding of myself. You know, I wasn't able to connect well with anyone, including myself. I was always living on the surface, finding happiness in my accomplishments and materialistic success. I was driven by the desire to accumulate more and more wealth. I would feel great after buying myself that dream car, but the high would fade, and I would once again feel empty inside. So, I would add another possession to the list, and the cycle would repeat itself. Just like cars, the girls in my life would come and go. And then my wife left me, and I couldn't figure out why. I thought I was keeping her happy with everything she wanted. But obviously, that wasn't enough. She had everything except me..." Jake's voice trailed off.

"And then what happened?" Maya asked.

"Then I met you, and I couldn't get over you. I lost interest in dating other girls. Something changed within me, and I decided to join a group and start past life regression therapy," Jake said. "Through the therapy, I learned why I struggled to connect with people. Tom explained it well to me - past life issues. I'm not sure if I fully buy into the concept, but Tom helped me become more mindful and engage in self-reflection to connect with myself. Once I could connect with myself, I was able to connect with others. I'm sure you understand, being a past life therapist yourself, Maya."

Maya nodded. "Yes, I understand. I'm glad it helped you."

"But that's not all, sweetie," Jake said. "In one session, I discovered that you're my soulmate. That's why I felt this deep and unusual connection with you. I couldn't see past that. Do you believe that we are soulmates?"

Maya looked away. "Jake, I know we have a spiritual connection, and I knew we had to meet in this life. But in what capacity or what may come out of it is something I don't know. No one has answers to such things, you know."

"Have you done a past life regression yourself?" Jake asked.

"Yes, I have," Maya replied. "But only my current path in this life was revealed to me, my spiritual path."

"Why?"

Maya's eyes sparkled as she began to share her discovery. "In the depths of my parents' old closet, I stumbled upon an ancient astrology chart. It is a cultural thing to create these celestial maps when a child is born. Curiosity got the better of me, and I delved into my own chart." A serene smile graced her lips as if she had glimpsed a secret beyond time itself. "But as I traced the lines and deciphered the symbols, I realized something extraordinary. The chart abruptly ceased after 29 years, as if the future had been veiled from sight."

Jake's brow furrowed, captivated by the mystery. "It stopped there. What does that signify?"

A gentle sigh escaped Maya's lips. "It could imply that the seers and scribes of old could not perceive beyond that point. Perhaps it suggests a fleeting existence, a life cut short. But you know, Jake," she smiled, "I don't worry about those things. I choose to live every day with joy, unburdened by the uncertainties of tomorrow."

Jake was genuinely worried. "But your health is sound, Maya. How can one simply fade away?"

"I do not dwell on such thoughts, my love. Each sunrise gifts me happiness, and I cherish the present moment. The future holds its secrets, and that's not ours to see."

Reluctantly, Jake bid farewell, his voice laced with a mixture of affection and unease. "Call you later, my love," he whispered, ending the call and gently placing the phone down.

Within Jake's heart, there was a feeling of sadness and concern, as if the mystery of Maya's revelation had woven itself into the very fabric of their connection.

When Jake called again, Maya was in the kitchen with her mom, who was busy preparing a delicious vegetarian curry for dinner. Jake, feeling unwell, was curled up in bed. His voice sounded strained and hoarse. "Baby, I'm sick. I think I might have caught Covid."

"Oh no! Are you sure, love? I'm so sorry to hear that. You must be feeling awful. Take good care of yourself." Maya walked over to her mother and gave her the phone. "Say hi to Jake, Mom," she said.

Her mom smiled politely and greeted Jake before returning the phone to Maya.

Taking the phone back, Maya asked, "Honey, do you have any Indian spices with you? I can send you a recipe for a detox tea that will help you recover in less than 48 hours."

"What's the recipe for this magical tea?" Jake asked.

"It has turmeric, ginger, lemon, cloves, and cardamom."

"I know the first three, but I have no idea what the last two are."

Maya hurried to the pantry to grab the spices and showed them to Jake through the phone. "Can you buy these and make the tea?"

Jake let out a sigh. "Baby, I'm too tired to even get out of bed. You can make it for me when you come here."

Maya retreated to her bedroom, gently closing the door behind her. "Oh, my poor baby, I wish I was there with you."

"What would you do if you were here, hun?"

Maya's voice softened with tenderness. "I would cuddle with you in bed, hug and kiss you, and take care of you."

Jake's voice grew husky as he replied, "Then do it now, my love."

"Okay, imagine me next to you, giving you all the love and comfort you need."

Jake shifted over, making room for her imaginary presence. "Gosh, that sounds so good. And then, my love, we would make passionate love."

"What's love, Jake?" she asked.

Jake pulled the blanket over himself. "Love is the feeling of wanting to be with someone every single day, to hold and hug them until the end of time. It's laughing and crying together, sharing all of life's joys and sorrows."

Maya blushed. "Do you like children?"

"Of course I do. I've always wanted a little girl."

Maya's eyes sparkled with delight. "We think so much alike. Do you know what I would want to name our daughter?"

"What, my love?"

"Tara," Maya replied softly. "Tara means star."

"I love the name, babe."

By now, Jake appeared visibly tired, and Maya thought it best to allow him some rest. She ended the call, leaving Jake to find comfort in his sleep.

Twenty-Three

"In vain, I have struggled. It will not do. My feelings will not be repressed. You must allow me to tell you how ardently I admire and love you."

— Pride And Prejudice by Jane Austen

Anna was preparing to go to work when she got a text from Lilly.

Hey, hope everything's going alright. Has John returned from his business trip?

Anna quickly replied He will be back this weekend.

Just checking in. How are things going between you two? Have you gotten over the funk? Lilly asked.

Anna texted back with a smile, "Yes, and yes!" She felt a beautiful sense of bliss and love.

Anna eagerly anticipated John's return, no longer questioning their relationship. Instead, she embraced the idea of letting it unfold naturally, allowing it to blossom and flourish on its own terms. "Just a few more days," she reminded herself, her excitement building as she began to plan a surprise welcome for him.

The flight arrived ahead of schedule. John swiftly retrieved his laptop and carrying bag and hurried towards the baggage area. Excitement filled his heart as he looked forward to meeting Anna. Upon reaching the baggage area, he spotted her eagerly waiting for him. With a joyful sprint, she rushed into his awaiting arms.

"I love you, John," Anna said. She wondered if it was the first time she had ever said it so loudly and clearly.

"I love you, babe, and I missed you so much," John replied as he kissed her.

Anna and John returned to her apartment, where she had already set the table for him. "I've prepared a delicious chicken biryani for you, hun. It's flavorful without being too spicy," Anna said as she began plating the dish.

John closed his eyes and inhaled the delightful aroma. "Mmm, it smells delicious."

After savoring their dinner together, they cozied up in front of a crackling fireplace, sharing warm hugs and tender kisses. Anna, with a sudden surge of excitement, made her way to the bedroom.

She returned, holding a beautifully wrapped gift in her hands. With a sparkle in her eyes, she handed it to John and asked him to open it.

John unwrapped the gift with care, revealing a tie adorned with elegant peacock designs. Alongside it was a small piece of paper decorated with hearts and a beautifully written poem. He began to read it.

"Your laughter

Created ripples.

In my tranquil dream

Your words of satire

Became my metaphor.

Ending at a crossroad

When the sunset

In your eyes

I found a garden.

Filled with butterflies.

And I made paper boats.

With dreams

And let it sail away.

In the currents of time

You had to come.

I asked for you.

Before I clad myself

In my human attire

Why did I choose?

This season of mine?

When do daffodils never bloom?

I could have

Asked the divine

To let you come in.

With the Robin

In the summer of my life

Time kept fleeting.

Were you late, my love?

Or time stood still for you.

My timeless love?"

Anna observed him closely as he read, and when he finally
finished, she couldn't contain her feelings. "I believed I had lost
my ability to write, but then you entered my life, and I
rediscovered my true self."

John gently placed the gift down and tenderly scooped Anna
into his arms, carrying her to the bedroom. "I have longed to hold
you close," he whispered. Leaning in, he kissed her passionately.

The following morning, as Anna prepared for work, the sound
of the ringing phone interrupted her. It was Ma calling. She
considered ignoring it, but in the end, she chose to answer at the
eleventh hour.

Anna was surprised to hear her Papa's voice on the other end
of the phone. "You are such a disgrace to our family!" he yelled.
"Do you have any idea what you've done? It's shameful! We never
imagined you would be involved in prostitution. We saw pictures

of you in a car, kissing and hugging a white man. Your mother couldn't bear it. She cried for a long time, devastated that she raised you to sink to this level. She was so heartbroken that she even contemplated taking her own life. Thankfully, we intervened and saved her. It was Alex who informed us about your involvement in this. He said you ruined his life, and now you're engaged in prostitution. I hope you realize the gravity of your actions." He abruptly ended the call.

Anna felt a sudden chill run down her spine. She sank to the floor, tears streaming down her face, overwhelmed by the weight of it all. She picked up her phone and called her workplace, her voice trembling as she explained that she wouldn't be able to come in that day. With no other solution in mind, she retreated to her bed, her eyes swollen from crying. The phone kept ringing, it was John, but she didn't bother to get up or answer it. At that moment, she felt like a lifeless body, still breathing.

After finishing his day at work, John had a feeling that something wasn't right. He couldn't shake off his concern for Anna, so he rushed over to her apartment. Despite ringing the doorbell repeatedly, there was no response. Growing increasingly anxious, he remembered the spare key Anna had given him. Relieved to find it, he unlocked the door and began searching for her. In the bedroom, he saw Anna lying in bed, visibly in deep pain, resembling a wounded animal. He climbed into the bed beside her, wrapping his arms around her. She began to sob, tearfully disclosing what had occurred.

"Alex is relentlessly attacking me, determined to make me give up," Anna said.

John looked into her eyes as he spoke. "I promise to take care of this and make sure nothing happens to you as long as I'm alive. Trust me, babe." He then went to the kitchen, opened a can of chicken soup, and warmed it. Returning with a bowl and spoon, he fed her the soup. He called Martha to inform her that he wouldn't be coming home because he couldn't leave Anna. That night, Anna slept in his arms, and he cradled her like a baby.

John reluctantly went to work the next day. He didn't want to leave Anna alone.

During lunch break, he called her and found her still in bed.

"I took a week off from work," Anna said. "I feel so broken, can't focus on work now."

"I'll take care of everything, okay?" John reassured her.

"I understand," Anna said. "I know you'll be busy for the next two days, but can you call me in the evening?"

"Yes, I'll call," John said.

"Don't worry about me, babe. I'll be fine," Anna reassured him.

"I've asked Lilly to come over tonight and stay with you for two days to make sure you're okay."

"That sounds great, John. Thank you"

It was around 6 p.m. when Lilly rang the doorbell. Anna was getting dinner ready for the two of them. The house smelled amazing, with the aroma of lemon rice and chicken tikka masala filling the air. Lilly took a deep breath, enjoying the rich spices that teased her senses. "Wow, looks like you're cooking up a feast for a whole village, girl!" she remarked.

Anna laughed. "I de-stress myself with cooking. Whenever I get super stressed, I cook like there's no tomorrow. Cooking is like an art, and the best part is you have some control over it. When life gets all chaotic and I feel like everything's falling apart, I just turn to cooking."

Anna served Lilly dinner and asked, "Hope you like it? John is a big fan of lemon rice and chicken tikka masala!"

"So you guys already started playing the house game, huh?" Lilly said.

Anna smiled. "It was going great, and then this happened, you know."

"So, Anna, let me get this straight. Your ex, Alex, had someone follow you and John, taking pictures of you kissing, and then sent those pictures to your parents? Am I understanding this correctly?" Lilly was a bit confused. "Honestly, it doesn't sound like a big deal to me."

"Nah, it's not like that, Lily," Anna said. "Pa called me from home and told me Mom overdosed after seeing the pictures. She was so upset, and Pa thinks I'm out here hustling."

"Prostitution? Is being in a relationship the same as prostitution? I don't get it." Lilly was quick to add.

"It's kinda hard to explain." Anna continued. "My folks knew some stuff that went down in my marriage. I didn't say much 'cause they didn't wanna hear it. I didn't tell them about the crazy mental and physical abuse I went through with Alex. So now they blame me. They think I didn't try hard enough to save my marriage. And now they're convinced I'm hooking up with random dudes."

Lilly finished her dinner and headed to the kitchen to rinse the plate. Anna tagged along right after her.

"Anna, let's grab some coffee tonight and chat more," Lilly said.

"I can't," said Anna. "I'm afraid."

"Afraid? Of what?" Lilly was curious.

"More people who are familiar with my parents will witness what happens next, and only God knows the outcome." Anna was visibly distressed.

"Anna, seriously, are you going to lock yourself up forever? Look, I get it; you're a psychologist and all, but sometimes, we all need to face the harsh truth. I know you don't care about Alex. You're just scared of what he might do next to get to your parents. He knows they're your weak spot, and you don't want them to get hurt. He knows all your buttons. There's only one way to put an end to this, Anna. You gotta sit down and have a heart-to-heart with your parents. You need to share your story with them, just like you did with us. They deserve to know. And let them know that you're in a relationship now and you're happy. It's up to them to accept it or not. Once you do that, you won't have to fear Alex ever again. Trust me." Lilly was convinced that was the only solution to this problem.

Anna sadly exclaimed, "How can I say all these on the phone when they live continents away?"

"You should then take some time off work and go home. Apply for FMLA and take maybe two months off. See your parents, talk to them, travel, and go on a healing journey. You need it. You need a break," Lilly said.

"What about John? I mean, I don't want this to affect our relationship."

"If you don't go and talk things out with your parents, you'll always be living in fear, you know? It's like being handcuffed, trapped in a prison in your own heart. Trust me, it's suffocating. Fear will ruin you and even ruin what you want: your relationship with John. You've got one option: face it head-on, get your closure, and then come back. John will understand, I promise," Lilly assured Anna.

Anna and Lilly were just about to go to sleep when John gave them a call. They could hear music and voices in the background, making it a bit difficult to hear him.

"Anna, just wanted to give you a call and see how you're doing, babe." John sounded a bit more serious than usual.

"I'm doing well, babe. Where are you?" Anna asked. "It sounds like you're in a really busy place."

I'm at a bar with Boris and Steven, hun! We've got some very serious business to take care of. I'll call you soon. Sleep well, okay?" John hung up.

Twenty-Four

*"A real friend is one who walks in when the rest of
the world walks out."*

— *Walter Winchell*

The local bar was getting busier every minute. Boris, John, and Steven found a table in a dimly lit area that offered a view of the bar.

"He will be here any minute," Boris explained.

"What does Alex look like?" John was curious.

Boris showed John a picture of Alex on his phone. "He always looks disheveled and has an odd affect," Boris said. "I talked to some trusted sources in the company, and they didn't have anything nice to say about him. They called him an oddball."

Inside the bar, there was lively music playing. A young couple sat on the left side while the bartender mixed a Long Island iced tea and chatted with them. Alex walked in, holding a laptop and with one end of his shirt hanging out. He went straight to the left corner where the young couple sat and said, "Hello there, that's my spot. Can you move?"

Whispers filled the air as people noticed Alex. One bartender looked at the server and said, "Uh-oh, trouble in paradise."

The young lady was taken aback by his request, more like a command, and asked, "I didn't know there were designated spots here.

"This is where I always sit, day after day. Move," he demanded, urging the young lady.

Sensing trouble, she politely stood up and relocated to the right side.

Alex took a seat at the bar and loudly requested, "Okay, amigo, give me my usuals."

The bartender skillfully prepared three chilled scotch on the rocks and served them to Alex, ready to be enjoyed.

In a matter of seconds, Alex downed all three drinks and asked for a few more. The man sitting on his right, who was enjoying a quiet evening with his wife, tried to reason with him, saying, "That's a bit too fast." Alex looked at him and replied, "This is my medicine." Soon, more people gathered around the bar and became attentive listeners.

"I need this now to sleep," Alex continued. "You know, she left me, my wife."

"I'm sorry to hear that. But drinking away and harming yourself is not the solution to the problem," the gentleman on the right side remarked.

By now, Alex was getting louder.

Boris nudged Steven and said, "Start the video recording."

Do you have any idea what that woman did to me, I mean my wife?

"Are you still married to her?" another attentive listener inquired as Alex's conversation began to captivate a growing audience.

" No, she left me. She is now painting the town red with a white boy," Alex added.

"She has the right to leave," remarked another guy.

"Says who? Till death do us part, that is what is written in the holy scriptures! This is the curse of modern society. I should have listened to my mother. She said from day one I should keep my wife under my control. I did for the most part, but I made one mistake that was allowing her to get that damn Job; Alex was now getting angrier by the minute, and the crowd was getting visibly upset".

"I gave it to her. I got pictures of her kissing and making it out with her white boy and sent them to her folks back in India. I said to them that their daughter has now become a prostitute"." He was now screaming at the top of his lungs, and everyone around him knew that Alex was no longer in control".

Someone from the crowd stepped forward and said, "You need serious help, bro."

Alex continued his rambling, saying, "She will be devastated and humiliated, maybe even pushed to the brink. But I won't stop there. I am planning an even bigger blow. I will share these pictures with everyone I know and post them on Facebook as well. She won't know where to turn". "The crowd was now completely silent. Everyone was taken aback by Alex's plan of revenge and the level of anger he had".

Someone finally spoke up, "You need to go home now."

People started whispering to each other. The manager approached Alex and said, "You have to leave."

Why should I leave when I'm paying for my drinks?

The manager said, "You're causing a disturbance. If you don't leave, we'll have to call the police."

"Alright, alright," he said as he quickly finished his last drink, placed the glass on the table, and left the bar.

The patrons exchanged wary glances, the weight of his bitter words still lingering in the room. The unpleasant words still hung in the air, leaving an indelible mark on the room. It was as if his presence had been a storm, leaving behind a trail of wreckage and raw emotions.

Some leaned in closer to their companions, seeking solace in the shared experience. Others turned their attention back to their drinks as if the liquid courage could shield them from the unsettling encounter. The bartender, whose hands had moments ago danced expertly over the array of bottles, now wiped down the bar with deliberate motions as if trying to erase the lingering echoes of Alex's tirade.

Outside, the city continued its ceaseless rhythm, oblivious to the turmoil that had just unfolded within the bar's walls. The distant sounds of traffic and the occasional laughter of passersby provided a stark contrast to the heaviness that still clung to the room.

John, Boris, and Steven, still in their corner booth, exchanged a series of subdued glances. Their faces were etched with a mixture of concern and disbelief, processing the gravity of what they had just witnessed.

In the midst of the aftermath, one could almost feel the collective sigh of the patrons, a communal reaction that they had weathered a storm together. It was a reminder of the resilience of the human spirit and the capacity to find strength in unity, even in the face of adversity.

As the minutes passed, the bar slowly resumed its familiar cadence.

As the heavy door swung shut behind Alex, a palpable sense of liberation settled over the bar, the air seeming to clear in his absence. The dimly lit bar, once charged with frenetic energy, now exhaled a collective breath as the heavy door swung shut behind Alex. The resounding thud seemed to echo through the space, sealing off the torrent of venomous words that had poured forth from him.

Laughter, though tentative, bubbled up from pockets of patrons, mingling with the low hum of tête-à-tête. The bartender resumed their rapid ballet of mixing drinks, the clinking of glass against the glass a reassuring metronome.

The night wore on, the bar gradually returning to its former self, albeit with a newfound air of cautious camaraderie. The neon lights continued to cast their vibrant radiance, painting the faces of those who remained with a gentle, almost forgiving light. And though the memory of Alex's vicious words would linger, the pliability of the human spirit prevailed, reminding them all that even in the murkiest moments, there was always the potential for light to return.

Outside, the city lights flickered a gentle glow on the pavement.

John turned to Boris and Steven, asking, "So, what's the plan now?"

Boris added, "No choice. We have to follow him home."

"Steven, can you handle cleaning up the files from his phone and laptop? Boris was wondering.

" I will need an hour for the complete cleanup," Steven answered.

We gotta stop him now before more damage is done. I got his address. We gotta follow him home. We don't have a choice but to use some scare tactics. I got my gun with me, but no violence, I promise. Okay with you, boss? He asked John.

"Got no choice," John replied.

They paid their bills and walked out of the bar.

We'll have to hold on a little longer before we make our way to his place. Boris insists that it needs to be just a tad darker.

They strolled towards a quaint sandwich and salad bar and ordered a couple of sandwiches.

You have all the videotape recordings, right, Steven? John asked.

"Yes, Boss, I have everything," he said.

"We will need it if we plan on taking legal action in the future," said John. "It's unfortunate what we witnessed. The saddest part is that physical abuse is easier to prove than mental abuse. I've seen many cases like this. The victim leaves, and these perpetrators show up in court, claiming loyalty and nonsense. Perpetrators of mental abuse often pretend to be loyal spouses who want to work things out, but they often ignore the toxic issue. Sometimes, it seems like they lack any insight into their actions, while other times, it feels like there's a thin line between sanity and insanity," Boris added.

"I can't even begin to fathom how Anna managed to tolerate this level of sheer madness," John exclaimed in utter disbelief.

"Time for a home visit and some real action," Boris said, and they stepped out to call an Uber.

The trio stepped into the waiting Uber, the soft hum of the engine providing a welcome contrast to the chaotic scene they had just left behind. The city's night sounds accompanied them, a symphony of distant traffic and muted conversations.

As the car wound its way through the city streets, John could not help but replay the events in his mind. The memory of Alex's venomous verses stayed, leaving a nasty palate in his mouth. It was a stark reminder of the darkness that could reside within even the most unassuming individuals.

Boris, seated beside him, remained deep in thought, his brow furrowed in contemplation. Steven, in the backseat, stared out of the window, lost in his own reflections. The heft of the meet hung heavy in the air, each of them grappling with the unsettling revelation.

The Uber pulled up to their destination, a modest apartment building nestled amongst the city's towering structures. They climbed out, the night air cool against their skin. The door clicked shut behind them, and they ascended the steps in silence.

Inside the apartment, the atmosphere was markedly different from the bar they had just left. Soft lighting cast a warm light, and the faint scent of fresh flowers permeated the air. It was a sanctuary, a place where they could momentarily escape the turmoil of the outside world.

They gathered in the open reception area, the events of the evening still weighing on their minds.

John broke the silence, his voice measured. "We need to be careful," he cautioned, his gaze fixed on his companions. "What we heard tonight... it's beyond anything I expected."

Boris nodded solemnly, his expression reflecting the gravity of the situation. "You're right," he agreed. "We stumbled upon something far darker than we anticipated."

Steven, his usually jovial demeanor replaced by a solemn resolve, spoke up. "We have a responsibility here. We cannot let this go unchecked. What Alex did... it's reprehensible."

In that solemn moment, as they stood in their shared refuge, John, Boris, and Steven exchanged determined looks that spoke volumes. Their eyes held a steady resolve, a shared understanding that went beyond the confines of their friendship. It was a bond forged in their shared commitment to justice, a promise they had made to themselves and to the world. They were resolute in their belief that doing what was right was not a choice but a duty. It was an unspoken pact that bound them together, a force that propelled them forward in the face of darkness. This commitment was the bedrock upon which their collective strength was built, a pillar that would support them through the challenges that lay ahead. They were more than friends; they were warriors in a battle for truth and justice, and they stood united, ready to face whatever came their way.

The night was cloaked in a shroud of shadows, punctuated only by the distant hum of city life. Steven, John, and Boris walked up to Alex's apartment. Its facade bore the wear and tear of urban existence, a silent witness to countless stories, both mundane and extraordinary.

With a determined exhale, Steven took the lead, striding forward to face the inevitable confrontation. He raised his hand to knock, his knuckles rapping against the door in a measured cadence.

"Delivery for Alex," he announced, his voice steady, though his heart raced in anticipation.

The door creaked open, revealing Alex, a figure swathed in shadows and apprehension. His eyes, once sharp and confident, now betrayed the glint of alcohol-induced haze. He swayed slightly, struggling to maintain his composure.

"Ah, the savior is here," he slurred, a bitter edge lacing his words. He extended an unsteady hand, a mocking gesture of hospitality.

"Anyone care to have a drink at my expense?" He erupted into raucous laughter, a sound that reverberated through the cramped apartment.

In the suffocating stillness, the tension was palpable, each heartbeat echoing like a drumroll of impending reckoning. The very walls of the apartment seemed to lean in as though conspiring to witness the inevitable clash of wills. Shadows danced nervously across the faded wallpaper, their silhouettes elongated and distorted by the dim light.

The air itself bore the weight of unspoken words, pregnant with the gravity of their collective plight. It was a charged pause, a moment stretched to its limits as if time itself held its breath. The creaking floorboards, usually silent sentinels of countless secrets, now groaned in reluctant anticipation, adding their voice to the symphony of anticipation.

Eyes darted between the players in this high-stakes confrontation, pupils dilated with a mix of apprehension and steely determination. Each face bore the lines of a battle-worn soldier, etched with scars both seen and unseen. Steven's grip on the camera tightened, his breath measured and deliberate, capturing every nuance, every twitch of muscle, every flicker of emotion.

The silence was peppered only by the distant city sounds, a muted backdrop to the impending storm. Outside, the urban symphony continued its ceaseless crescendo — the distant wail of sirens, the muffled bass of music from a neighboring building, and the rhythmic shuffle of footsteps on the pavement below. But within those four walls, a different sonata played, one composed of raw emotion, tangled motives, and the unyielding pursuit of justice.

It was a moment suspended in time, a fragile equilibrium before the inevitable rupture. The very foundations of the room seemed to pulse with the heartbeat of their collective resolve. Each second hung like a precipice, teetering on the edge of an irrevocable shift.

And then, as if guided by an invisible hand, the storm broke.

The words, when they came, were a thunderclap, shattering the fragile stillness. The confrontation unfurled, emotions and accusations spilling forth like torrents of rain after a long, oppressive drought. The room, once a vessel of stifling quiet, now echoed with the clamor of their truths, a tempest of release.

Unsteady on his feet, Alex lurched forward, approaching John with a venomous intensity. His words spat like acid, each syllable a searing accusation.

"You think you can save her," he sneered, his laughter tinged with malice. "Too bad, it's over. I have sent your X-rated pictures to everyone, and I plan to send them to more. She is screwed, and you are doomed."

As the tirade continued, Alex's anger swelled into an inferno of rage and desperation. His voice crescendo-ed, echoing off the walls in a harrowing symphony of torment.

"She will kill herself," he roared, the threat hanging heavy in the air.

"And if she doesn't trust me, I will kill her."

In the shadows, Steven stood like a silent sentinel, his presence barely registering amidst the chaos that unfolded. His eyes, sharp and unyielding, were fixated on the scene before him, every movement and every word etching itself onto the canvas of his memory.

The camera, an extension of his being, was cradled in his hands, its lens a watchful eye, its shutter a relentless witness. He operated with a precision born of years of practice, adjusting settings with deft, practiced movements. Each frame he captured was a piece of the puzzle, a fragment of the damning tapestry they were weaving against Alex. Every click of the shutter was a beat in the rhythm of justice, a symphony of evidence that would sing loud and clear in the courts.

His breaths were measured, an unspoken cadence that matched the ebb and flow of the confrontation. He was a maestro of the visual, attuned to the nuances that spoke volumes beyond words. The play of light and shadow on the faces of the players, the tension that coiled in their bodies, the flicker of desperation in Alex's eyes — all were captured with a precision that bordered on artistry.

Time seemed to warp around him, distilling into fleeting moments frozen in the frame. He was both participant and observer, his detachment a shield against the emotional tempest that raged around him. The camera was his anchor, grounding him in the purpose of their mission.

As the verbal onslaught reached its crescendo, Steven's fingers danced across the camera's buttons, ensuring no detail escaped his scrutiny. Each damning word was a brick in the fortress they were constructing, a bulwark against the tide of Alex's malevolence. He was acutely aware of the weight of responsibility that rested on his shoulders, the knowledge that the images he captured would be instrumental in delivering justice.

In that charged atmosphere, Steven's presence was a silent reassurance to his comrades. They knew that every moment of this confrontation was being meticulously documented and that their cause was being immortalized in pixels and frames. His unwavering focus was a testament to his dedication, a promise that their fight would not be in vain.

And when the storm finally abated, when the echoes of confrontation faded into the ether, Steven lowered the camera with a sense of quiet accomplishment. The evidence was secure, a fortress of truth that would stand against the onslaught of lies. He turned to his companions, a nod of affirmation passing between them. They had faced the storm and emerged stronger for it, armed with the indomitable power of irrefutable proof.

Then, as if a spark ignited the night, Boris rose from the periphery, a figure of calculated resolve. In his hand gleamed cold steel, a gun glinting in the muted light. "Give me the phone," he demanded, his voice a low growl that brooked no argument.

In that pivotal moment, fear coursed through Alex's veins, a visceral sensation that seized him in its merciless grip. The veneer of bravado that had shielded him now shattered like fragile glass, leaving him exposed and vulnerable. His once steely resolve now gave way to trembling uncertainty, his bravado reduced to trembling uncertainty.

His fingers, once nimble and assured, now fumbled with the phone, their movements erratic and uncoordinated. They betrayed the trembling of his entire being, the physical manifestation of the terror that held him captive. The device, once an extension of his power, now felt like an anchor dragging him down.

The phone slipped from his grasp, and he watched it fall into the waiting hand of Boris, a surrender of more than just a piece of technology. It was a concession of authority, a symbolic transfer of control. The device, now in Boris's possession, seemed to radiate a quiet authority, a testament to the shifting balance of power within the cramped apartment.

As he stood there, his chest rising and falling with rapid breaths, Alex could feel the weight of his actions pressing down on him. The consequences loomed, dark and foreboding, casting a long shadow over his once-secure world. He was now at the mercy of those he had sought to manipulate, a prisoner of his own malice.

Every sound seemed amplified in the stillness—the sharp intake of breath, the rustle of fabric, the low hum of the city beyond. It was a symphony of dread, a cacophony that underscored the gravity of the moment. Alex's gaze darted between the figures before him, seeking an escape that eluded him.

The room, once his fortress of control, now seemed to close in around him, its walls imbued with a palpable tension. The air itself seemed to pulse with the weight of impending judgment. He was adrift in a sea of his own making, the currents of fear threatening to pull him under.

In that cramped apartment, fear was a living, breathing entity, wrapping its icy fingers around Alex's heart. It whispered of consequences and retribution, a chilling reminder of the reckoning that awaited him. He was no longer the puppeteer, but the puppet, strings severed, and control wrested from his grasp.

As the seconds stretched on, the realization settled in — a pivotal shift had occurred, a seismic change in the dynamic of power. Alex was no longer the puppeteer, but the puppet, strings severed, and control wrested from his grasp. In that small, suffocating space, the balance had irrevocably tipped, and he stood on the precipice of a reckoning he could no longer evade.

"Boris," John's voice cut through the tension, steady and measured. "Have him log in to his computer."

Boris nodded, his eyes never leaving Alex. The computer screen flickered to life, casting an eerie glow on Alex's contorted face. With a sense of grim purpose, Steven took control, his fingers dancing across the keyboard like a maestro orchestrating a symphony.

Files were deleted and erased from existence with a few keystrokes. The digital remnants of Alex's malevolence vanished into the void, leaving no trace of the weapons he wielded against John and his beloved.

As the final keystroke fell, a silence settled over the apartment, a vacuum of sound in the wake of chaos. The mission was accomplished, and the battlefield was reclaimed.

They turned to leave, the weight of their collective resolve propelling them forward. John, his voice a blade of steel, addressed Alex for the first time. "All your threats, all your cruelty—it's all here, documented, evidence against you. Under section..." He cited legal statutes, each word a testament to the inexorable force of justice. "You're looking at half your life behind bars."

The reality hung in the air, a specter of consequences too grave to ignore. The choice was clear and stark in its simplicity. "You have one option," John concluded, his gaze unwavering. "Leave this city for good or face the consequences."

They left, the door closing behind them with a finality that echoed through the corridor. The night swallowed them whole, absorbing their steps into its silent embrace.

Days passed, and a tapestry was woven with threads of apprehension and cautious hope. In a clandestine meeting, Boris delivered the news like a messenger of fate. "Alex has left the city," he reported, his voice a solemn confirmation of their victory.

The city skyline stretched before them, a canvas of endless possibilities. The battle had been fought, and in its wake, a semblance of peace emerged.

Twenty-Five

"No one ever told me that grief felt so like fear."

— *C. S. Lewis*

It was Sunday, and surprisingly, it rained heavily. John rushed to see Anna after work. He hadn't seen her in two days. When John entered, Anna quickly grabbed a towel and dried his wet hair. John then sat on the sofa and invited Anna to join him.

"Anna, guess what? I've got some great news for you! Your worst nightmare is officially over. You don't have to worry about Alex anymore." John was so confident when he said it.

"What happened?" Anna asked, fear returning to her face.

"Anna, remember that night when you called? I was hanging out with Steven and Boris at the bar. We ended up following Alex to his apartment. Surprisingly, it wasn't that hard. He was wasted and just blabbering nonsense. Steven hacked into his computer and phone and deleted all the pictures. So he won't be able to find them again. And we made it clear that there'd be serious consequences if he ever tried to blackmail you again. Trust me, it's all sorted now." John sounded so relieved.

"""

"I'm sorry you had to go through this because of me." Anna gave John a big hug. She walked to the window. "It won't be over, John, until I put a stop to it. He knows I'm living in fear of my parents finding out and how it will affect them. There's only one way out of this: I have to go home and have a conversation with my parents. First, I need to explain what happened with my marriage and how much I suffered. I must tell them that if I had stayed, I would be dead by now. Then, I'll tell them about you. I'll say that I met a kind man, and we are in a relationship, and I have nothing to hide. I am in a relationship, and it's not prostitution." Anna almost smiled at this revelation.

"Think they'll get it?" John asked.

"They might or they might not; it's really up to them. But once I do that, I won't be afraid of Alex or anyone anymore." Anna spoke with more determination. "I gotta do it, John. I'm gonna apply for my FMLA and take about three months off."

"So, wait, you're telling me you'll be gone for three months?" John wasn't too thrilled about it.

"I gotta do it. I don't have a choice anymore. If I stick around, this fear will creep in and wreck me, and then it'll spread like wildfire and wreck us and our relationship," Anna sat down next to John.

"I gotta start getting used to a life without you, Anna, and it's gonna be tough. I know it's not forever, but it's gonna be really hard for me." John was visibly upset.

"There's something else I wanted to tell you, John. Please don't rush into conclusions. Just listen to what I have to say. You know, we got into our relationship too quickly. It felt right then, and it still feels right now. But I need to be sure. I want to take some time while I'm away to think things through more clearly. I want to know if what I feel and what we have is love and not just a passing infatuation. So, I need some space and time to figure it out. I'll text you occasionally while I'm gone, but we won't communicate as much as we used to. I want you to reflect on this, too." Anna spoke softly.

"Are you implying that we should end our relationship? Is all of this because of what Alex did?" John's anger was palpable.

"I didn't suggest ending our relationship, John. I just need some space to reflect and be on my own. I don't want to repeat past mistakes." Anna was now tearful.

John paced the room, his face filled with obvious distress. Thoughts eluded him, tangled in the chaos of his mind, unable to find clarity. "Okay, do as you wish, Anna," he replied concisely.

"You're struggling because your abandonment issues are triggering you," Anna tried to reason.

"No, it's not. I'm not an overthinker. I wanted our relationship to develop naturally. Yes, maybe we rushed into it, but as you said, it felt right then, and it still feels right now." John looked tired.

"Can I get the dinner ready, John?" Anna tried to alleviate the tension and sadness in the air.

"I am not hungry. I want to leave now. Let me consider it. Please give me some time, okay?" John casually hugged Anna and left her house.

The following day, Anna went to her workplace and completed the FMLA paperwork for three months. It was already nearing the end of July. After that, she sent a text message to Lilly.

I'm taking your advice and heading home, Lilly, she texted.

Lilly texted back, how did John react?

Not good, but he will come around, Anna said.

Okay, please keep me updated. Goodbye for now.

Anna anxiously awaited John's call the following day, but it never came. A profound sadness enveloped her, yet within that sorrow, a remarkable strength began to arise. It was from this newfound strength that wisdom and enlightenment were ultimately born.

It was way past midnight when the doorbell rang. "It's me, Anna," John said. "I couldn't sleep. I want to talk to you."

They proceeded to sit on the sofa, and Anna rested her face against John's chest.

"I have considered what you want, and although I am not pleased, I understand. I am willing to wait for you, not only for two months but for a lifetime, if necessary," John stated.

"Have you heard about the invisible red string? Anna asked. "It is an ancient Chinese proverb that says that an invisible red thread connects those who are destined to meet regardless of time, place, or circumstance. The thread may stretch or tangle, but it will never break! If it's meant to be, it will be. When I am gone, look within. Look in your heart. If you can find me there, feel me, then that means that I am energetically connected with you, John. You don't need to look at the external circumstances to get solutions to our internal conflicts at times. Our answers will come from our higher self or super consciousness."

"I will try, baby." He smiled.

The next few days flew by, consumed by Anna's frantic preparations for her upcoming trip. Finally, she secured her flight tickets for the end of August. John, though inwardly torn, put on a brave face, determined not to let his true emotions show. Deep down, he knew he was going to miss her.

The end of August had finally arrived, marking the day for Anna's departure. As John and Lilly drove her to the airport, the crisp air of fall whispered stories of change and growth. It was a season of shedding the old and leaving behind what no longer served her highest good.

"Lilly, make sure you take care of John," Anna reminded Lilly.

"He will be fine, gal. You do what you need to do," Lilly comforted Anna.

John helped her with the bags, and they headed to the check-in together. Anna gave hugs to Lilly and then to John. Anna and John embraced for a while. Just before Anna went to the final security check-in, she pulled out a gift from her bag and gave it to John.

"There's a small gift for you in here, along with a letter," she said. "Read it in a few days."

John held the gift in his hand, pulled Anna into his arms one more time, and gave her a kiss. As John watched Anna walk away, his heart sank, and old fears of being left behind started creeping in.

Twenty-Six

"I don't want to lose you in my life. You are the stars in my sky and the sun in my world. You are the reason I survive."

– Unknown

As the seasons shifted, painting New York City in the vibrant hues of fall, Jake and Maya found their hearts entwined more deeply with each passing day. Jake felt a sense of belonging, as if he were an integral part of Maya's family. He affectionately referred to Maya's parents as Amma and Achen and her cousin as brother Siddh. Their phone calls began to transcend mere conversations, evolving into cherished moments of familial connection. Yet, amidst this growing bond, Maya and Jake still cherished their private exchanges, nurturing the flame of their love.

The day Maya had eagerly anticipated had finally arrived - Onam, a celebration brimming with joy and traditions. Maya was wearing a very traditional dress; her skirt boasted golden borders, while her midriff-baring top exuded a subtle allure. As she delicately selected her bangles, Jake's call interrupted her preparations.

Maya's excitement overflowed, causing her to dance, sing, and twirl, seeking Jake's opinion on her attire. His smile spoke volumes, affirming her beauty and radiance. Pointing to the blue shawl draped over her shoulders, Maya asked Jake in a playful voice, "Love this one, or that one, the red one over there."

With a gaze filled with adoration, Jake responded, "The blue one looks absolutely fabulous on you, my love!"

Maya's heart fluttered with delight as she decided to keep the blue shawl.

A mischievous glimmer danced in Jake's eyes as he playfully asked, "Any chances of rain, hun?"

Maya, unaware of his hidden intentions, innocently replied, "Nope, I hope it doesn't rain. We have a Pookalam outside that I'll show you in a minute, followed by traditional dances and a grand feast called Sadya, served on banana leaves. I can't wait to share it all with you."

Jake pondered for a moment before revealing his mischievous plan. "Hey, hun, before you show me the festivities, I want you to take off that blue shawl and wear the red one. You know, just to make sure."

Maya complied, removing the blue shawl, ready to don the red one. However, Jake interrupted her, instructing her to turn around. Maya obliged, and Jake whispered, "For my eyes only, stay that way for a while."

Maya erupted into laughter, realizing Jake's playful intentions. "You naughty boy, so this was your plan all along," she exclaimed, her laughter echoing through the room.

But soon, the longing in Jake's voice became palpable. "This separation is becoming unbearable, babe. I can't bear to be away from you any longer. I want to come to India, and together, we'll return. I want you to move in with me."

Maya's mind whirled, trying to process the weight of Jake's words. "Amma and Achen wouldn't allow me to live with a man without marrying him, love."

Without a moment's hesitation, Jake declared, "Then marry me."

The gravity of his words hung in the air, leaving Maya speechless, her heart pounding with a mix of emotions. Searching for words, Maya finally managed to ask, "Are you serious?"

"I have longed to ask this question for so long, uncertain of the right moment. But now, I am certain. I want to marry you, Maya."

Her laughter mingled with disbelief. "So, you want us to get married without the formalities of dating or going out? It sounds more like an arranged marriage."

Jake's unwavering gaze met hers, and he replied, "So be it. I am willing to marry you in the way of arranged marriages."

Maya found herself at a loss for words. "Let me talk to Amma and Achen," she said.

After the Onam celebrations came to an end, Maya knew it was time to have a crucial conversation with Amma and Achen. Finding Amma in the kitchen, cleaning up after the festivities, Maya embraced her, her heart brimming with anticipation. She whispered, "I need to talk to you and Achen."

Achen, drawn by the aroma of freshly brewed coffee, joined them in the kitchen, pulling up a chair to sit.

Maya took a deep breath and mustered the courage to share her decision. "I want to marry Jake before I return, and I am certain of my choice."

A profound silence enveloped the room as Amma and Achen absorbed Maya's words. Then, breaking the silence, Achen asked, "Where and when?"

Maya's eyes sparkled with excitement as she replied, "Jake is willing to come to India, and we want to have a small Hindu wedding here, with just our immediate families for now."

Amma and Achen's expressions revealed no surprise; they had sensed this moment. Finally, Achen spoke. "Let us then find a suitable date in the month of November. It's only two months away."

Maya's heart soared with joy, unable to contain her excitement. She couldn't wait to share the news with Jake, knowing that their love had received the blessing of her parents.

Achen, determined to find the perfect date for Maya and Jake's wedding, sought the guidance of the local astrologer, Ramaswamy. With a sense of urgency, Achen explained the situation and requested a suitable date in November.

Ramaswamy, an experienced astrologer, assured Achen that he could fulfill his request. "I can make that happen, sir," he replied respectfully. "In fact, I have Maya's astrological profile from years ago in my records, so I won't need her birthdate or time of birth."

After a few days, Ramaswamy arrived at Maya's residence, his expression somber. He kept his words concise, stating,

"November 11th is a good day for weddings." His gaze shifted away as if burdened by something unspoken.

Maya's heart leaped with joy upon hearing the news. "I have to call Jake," she said, her voice filled with an indescribable joy. "I'll ask him to come at least on the 8th of November so he can rest, and we can prepare for the wedding on the 11th."

When Jake called that night, Maya's heart soared with joy. She could hardly contain her excitement as she shared the news with him. "Love, we have a date, 11-11," she exclaimed, her voice filled with happiness.

"Perfect," he replied. "darling, I discussed it with my family, and although they were a bit apprehensive, they are happy for me. I promised them that at some point in the future, we could have an American wedding, too. Are you okay with that?"

"More than happy, love. I am completely okay with that. Our love is what matters the most, and I am excited to celebrate it in any way we choose."

"I can't wait, Maya. I'm thrilled to be a part of the simple wedding at home. The Pooja, exchanging garlands, and all the traditional elements sound wonderful."

Their shared excitement and anticipation for their upcoming wedding filled the air as they both realized that their love would be celebrated in a beautiful and meaningful way.

The next two months flew by in a whirlwind of wedding preparations for Maya and Jake. Maya poured her heart into designing their wedding attire, ensuring that every detail reflected their love and unique style. Meanwhile, they eagerly discussed their future living arrangements. Maya was thrilled to know that Lilly would be coming to India for the wedding as well.

Jake, excitedly sharing his plans, showed Maya pictures of beautiful cottages by the sea. Maya's eyes sparkled with delight as she envisioned their future home.

"A small cottage by the sea, with white furniture and white curtains," she said, her voice filled with dreams and happiness. "I can't wait."

Twenty-Seven

"I wish you to know that you have been the last dream of my soul."

— Charles Dickens, A Tale of Two Cities

The days that came after were the most challenging for John. In the absence of Anna, he reverted to his former self. The old John resurfaced, leaving his heart feeling empty once more. He suppressed all his emotions, whether they were positive or sorrowful. The only time he allowed himself to be vulnerable and truly feel was when Noah was present. Martha quietly witnessed this regression and felt powerless in her attempts to assist John.

Almost a month had elapsed, and John found himself at his office when he received yet another text from Lilly. He had ignored her previous messages, but this time, he decided to open it. The words on the screen read, John, you haven't responded to any of my previous texts. Jake and I are genuinely worried about you.

Feeling compelled to reply, John typed back, I'm okay. I just miss Anna so much. There has been no communication from her.

Lilly's response came swiftly. Give her time, John. Don't rush things. We can catch up over coffee sometime, alright?

John sent a brief thank-you text and suddenly remembered something. After returning home from bidding farewell to Anna, he had been so heartbroken that he hadn't even opened the gift she had given him. Now, curiosity consumed him. He couldn't wait to get home and uncover its contents.

"What could be inside?" John wondered, but the mere thought of the gift injected a glimmer of hope into his weary heart.

Late that night, after tucking Noah into bed, John retrieved the gift and carefully unwrapped it. Inside, he discovered a stunning leather bracelet held together with a steel plate that boldly displayed the word "trust." Intrigued, he unfolded the accompanying letter and began to read Anna's words:

"Go deep within

Seek that flame.

That's you.

Align your soul.

With mine

Hold my hand.

Let's sit on a star.

In silence

In the deep blue

In the infinite paradise

Ask my soul.

Would I ever hurt you?

What do you feel, my love?

Now, let's twirl around the moon.

Soaking in the silver beams

Come deeper with me.

To my soul garden

What do you feel, my love?

Do you see your radiance in my

eyes?

Can you see what I can see?

The colors of your rainbow

Your light

Lighting my dark.

Dance with me

Through all my lives

Wear any attire!

Can you find me yet again?

In a crowd?

And know me like you know

yourself?

I have walked with you through many

lives.

What do you feel, my love?

I see you like a radiant light.

A fragment of myself, a fragment of

divine

And yet you doubt me.

What do you feel, my love?

I feel your joy, and I feel your pain.

I feel it in moments.

Far and within

The divine chord

That is binding us.

It will never fade with time.

What do you feel, my love?

She drew a heart, and under that, she inscribed, "Love yourself enough to trust yourself, my love, and in doing so, you will learn to trust me and trust in us."

Tears welled up in John's eyes as he held the bracelet close to his heart. As he gently placed the bracelet on his wrist, John felt a surge of strength and resilience. He knew that, in time, he would learn to trust himself and trust in their love again.

Every time John glanced at the bracelet, the word "trust" served as a constant reminder of Anna's wisdom. He couldn't help but ponder her words, realizing that trusting himself meant embracing his emotions fully.

"Anna said I had to trust myself first," John thought aloud. "That means I have to trust my emotions. I need to delve deep within myself and untangle my emotions. I must identify the ones that align with my current reality and the ones that stem from past traumas, coloring my present. And I have to let go of the trauma-based emotions and replace them with more positive ones rooted in trust."

As he continued to reflect, John felt a sense of determination growing within him. He knew that every day presented an opportunity to dig deeper into himself, to analyze and discard the emotions that no longer served him. "I have to be brave," John whispered to himself. "I need to confront my past traumas and acknowledge their impact on my present state. Only then can I let go of the emotions that hold me back and make space for new, vibrant emotions that paint a rainbow in my heart?"

With each passing day, John committed himself to this transformative journey. He would sit in quiet contemplation, examining his emotions and their origins. Sometimes, he would engage in conversations with himself, asking probing questions and seeking understanding.

"Why do I feel this way?" John would ask himself. "Is this emotion rooted in my present reality, or is it a remnant of my past?"

Through this process of self-analysis, John began to untangle the complex web of emotions within him. He learned to identify the emotions that were no longer serving him and consciously release them. In their place, he anchored the emotions that brought him joy, peace, and a renewed sense of trust.

As he continued to dig deeper into himself, John felt a profound shift taking place. The bracelet on his wrist became a symbol of his commitment to this ongoing journey of self-discovery and self-trust.

Twenty-Eight

"Whenever I miss you, I look at my heart. Because it's the only place I can find you."

— Unknown

It had been over a month since Anna left, and John was really missing her. They hadn't been in contact at all, and that was the hardest part for him.

The days stretched into weeks, and the weeks into a seemingly endless expanse of time without Anna. John's once steadfast heart now felt like fragile glass, teetering on the edge of shattering into a million irreparable pieces. The empty space she left behind in his life seemed to echo with the haunting absence of her laughter, her touch, and the warmth of her presence.

Every morning, he would wake up and reach instinctively for the side of the bed where she used to lay, only to be met with the harsh reality of empty sheets and cold linens. The apartment, once filled with the vibrant energy of their shared existence, now seemed cavernous and suffocating.

John's days were marked by a dull ache that seemed to settle in his chest, a constant reminder of the void Anna's absence had left behind. He tried to fill the hours with work, with hobbies, with anything that might distract him from the gnawing emptiness, but it was futile. His mind kept drifting back to her, to the memories they had created together, and to the promises of a future that now felt uncertain.

The nights were the hardest. Alone in the silence, the weight of her absence pressed down on him like a leaden cloak. He would lie in bed, staring at the ceiling, his thoughts a chaotic swirl of longing and doubt. He missed the sound of her breathing, the soft rustle of her movements as she slept beside him. The bed felt too big, too cold, too empty.

John's once unshakeable confidence wavered, replaced by a gnawing anxiety that ate at him from the inside out. He questioned himself, wondering if he had done enough if he had shown Anna just how much she meant to him. The uncertainty gnawed at him, a constant refrain in the back of his mind.

Yet, amidst the ache and the longing, there was a glimmer of hope. John clung to the belief that this separation was temporary, a necessary step in their individual journeys toward growth and self-discovery. He reminded himself that love was not confined by physical proximity, that it could transcend distance and time.

And so, John took each day as it came, learning to navigate the ebb and flow of his emotions. He allowed himself to feel the depth of his love for Anna, to acknowledge the pain of her absence, and to find strength in the belief that their connection was enduring. In the quiet moments before sleep claimed him, he whispered his hopes to the universe, trusting that, in time, they would be reunited.

As the days turned into weeks, John sought solace in the routines they had once shared. He visited their favorite spots, the places where their laughter had echoed, and their dreams had taken flight. He could almost hear her voice in the rustle of leaves, feel her presence in the soft breeze that caressed his skin.

He poured his heart into letters, scribbling down his innermost thoughts and feelings, sealing them with a promise of love that transcended the miles between them. Each word was a tether, a lifeline that stretched across the vast expanse, reaching out to Anna, hoping that she could feel the echo of his heart beating in time with hers.

In the midst of his longing, John discovered a newfound appreciation for the beauty that surrounded him. The world seemed to shimmer with a vibrancy he had never noticed before. The colors were more vivid, the sunsets more breathtaking, and the songs of birds more melodious. It was as if the world was conspiring to remind him that even in the absence of Anna, life continued to unfold in all its wondrous glory.

Yet, there were moments of darkness when doubt would creep in like a persistent shadow. John grappled with the fear that perhaps this separation was a harbinger of an ending rather than a pause in their story. The thought of a life without Anna was a specter he couldn't bear to face, a void that threatened to swallow him whole.

As the days turned into weeks, John found a semblance of healing in the small moments of connection that bridged the gap between them. He would send messages into the digital ether, pouring his heart into every word, hoping that they would find their way to Anna, a beacon of his love in the vast expanse of the virtual world.

It was a Friday, and after finishing a business meeting, John met up with his friends Boris and Steven. They decided to grab some Indian food to satisfy their hunger. They walked to a nearby Indian restaurant and decided to take a stroll through the Indian street afterward. Along the way, they stopped to grab a warm cup of filter coffee.

On the weekend, John decided to take his son Noah to the nearby bookstore. They spent some time there, with John reading stories to Noah. On their way out, John spotted an Indian cookbook and decided to grab it.

Later that evening, during dinner, John asked Martha, "Do you know how to cook Indian food?"

Martha burst into laughter, finding it amusing that John seemed to be interested in all things Indian. She jokingly asked, "What's with all this Indian stuff, John? Indian food, an Indian cookbook, and even getting me different masala packs. You're missing Anna, aren't you?"

John smiled, realizing that Martha had noticed his recent fascination with Indian culture. At that moment, John couldn't help but think, "I can't separate her from myself anymore. She has become a part of my inner being."

And then, like a ray of sunlight breaking through the clouds, putting an end to his arduous wait, John's heart leaped with joy as he finally received a message from Anna.

My dearest love,

I looked within my heart all these days, and
I found you there every day, as close to me
as always. I know you are there, and I know

nothing has changed between us. I feel so
energetically connected with you now more
than befo   re. So, here, I am going to write to
you about everything that   has   happened
since I boarded the flight.

I arrived in Cochin early in the morning.
Surprisingly, it wasn't raining. I had hoped
to experience the monsoons, but the air
was dry and cool instead.   I decided to take
an airport cab to go home. As I traveled on
the road for about an hour, the sun started
to peek through the clouds. I rolled down
my window and could see the familiar roads
and streets. Not much seemed to have
changed. The cab driver and   I made a quick
stop by the road to grab a hot cup of coffee.
I sat under a thatched roof at a coffee place
and enjoyed my coffee along with two idlis.
There were only a few cars passing by.

Strangely, I didn't feel nervous at all. I felt
a sense of calm w   ithin me.

We reached home at around 7:30 a.m. I told
the driver to pull over at the end of the
small lane that leads to my house. I took
my bag and walked towards my home. The
path was still narrow, with wire fences on
both sides. The paddy fields on eithe   r side
stretched far and wide. I noticed that it
was almost time for the harvest. A few
minutes later, I reached the concrete steps
and climbed up to the courtyard.

And that's when everything I had expected
didn't happen. I thought they   , Ma and
Pappa,   would both come out and tell me to
leave right away. I was prepared for my dad
and mom to insult me nonstop. I had even
mentally prepared myself to face these
challenges head   - on.

But at the final step that led to the courtyard, I saw Ma. She was spreading red chilies on a bamboo mat, trying to dry them under the scorching sun. As I watched her, tears started to flow from my eyes. At that moment, I felt like the little Anna I had left behind. Without even realizing it, I called out to Ma. She turned around, her eyes locking onto mine, and then she rushed towards me, her arms open wide. We embraced tightly, our tears flowing freely as we held each other. Amidst our tears and kisses, she lovingly repeated, "My daughter, my daughter."

Finally, when we both felt ready to speak, I spoke softly, "Ma, I came here to explain." To my surprise, she responded, "This is your home. What are you talking about?" She led me inside and began preparing breakfast. I stood behind her, wrapping my arms around her, and asked, "Where is Pappa? He was so angry with me after he saw the pictures." Ma turned to me and calmly said, "It's okay, babe. Everything will be alright." Tears welled up in my eyes once again as I questioned Ma, "Why did you take all those pills?" Ma brushed it off and replied, "Come, dear, have your breakfast. It was just a momentary thing."

We settled on two small wooden stools and sipped our chai. Shortly after, Papa entered the kitchen for his morning tea. He glanced at me, clearly taken aback, but surprisingly, he simply nodded and said, "Feed her well she has lost a lot of weight." He quickly grabbed his chai and left. As he walked away, I noticed him wiping away a tear with his white shawl.

Ma said she wanted to give food to the cows, so I went with her to the barn. I asked Ma where Lakshmi was, one of the oldest cows on our farm. Ma replied, asking me what I was thinking, as Lakshmi had passed away many years ago. She then pointed to Rukmini and said that she was Lakshmi's baby.

On our way back, Ma pointed to the chicken coop and reminded me of the time when I used to feed the chickens with half a sack of rice. It was one of my favorite activities. I would be so absorbed in a book that I wou ld use my other hand to feed the chickens with rice grains.

Ma wanted to make some homemade shampoo called "Thali" because she thought my hair had become dry and brittle. We walked further up the hill , and Ma collected some hibiscus leaves for the shampoo. When we returned to the house, Pa was sitting on the veranda, reading the newspaper. He was sitting on Grandpa's old chair and was completely engrossed in the news. He briefly looked up at me and then went back to reading. Ma sat down on the steps of the veranda and asked me to sit on the step below.

She untied my hair and ran her fingers through it, feeling the thickness of some strands. Then she expressed concern, saying, "Anna, you haven't been taking care of yourself." She began applying hot coconut oil infused with spices and curry leaves to my scalp. Both Ma and Pa were present, so I thought it was the right time to talk about Alex.

I mustered the courage and said, "Ma, no, I didn't take care of myself for years. I couldn't, Ma. I was mistreated by Alex and his family. I constantly felt like I was walking on eggshells. Alex would yell at me

all the time, and occasionally, he would physically hurt me. I thought that if I did things right or better next time, maybe he wouldn't scream, yell, or hit me. But no matter what I did, Ma, it was never enough.
I still got hurt. He would take all my paychecks and only give me $10 a day for my expenses. He wanted control over everything. I reached a point where I couldn't even think for myself, Ma. And if I had stayed, I believe I would have died." By then, I couldn't hold back my tears any longer.

At first, I was crying, then I started wailing, and eventually, I fell into Ma's lap and cried uncontrollably. Ma kept stroking my hair, and she was crying too. Pa came over, held my face in his hands, and kissed my forehead. We all sat there, feeling shattered but still holding onto hope.

In many ways, I would say that was one of the happiest days of my life. I was finally able to mend a broken relationship and start heal ing some of the oldest and deepest wounds in my heart. I felt a sense of joy after that. Now, there was one more important topic I wanted to discuss with them: our love story. However, I decided to save that conversation for another day.

After lunch, the three of us got into Pa's Mahindra Jeep and started our journey to Idukki. It was a three - hour trip filled with lively conversation. However, neither Pa nor Ma mentioned the pictures that Alex had sent of us. I wanted to bring it up, but I also wanted to g ive us some time to heal.

During the drive, Pa showed me different parts of his estate in Idukki and expressed his desire for me to inherit it. He mentioned that the other part would be more for

Naina. I suggested that they could write it all to Naina instead. However, Ma interrupted and said something that made me feel anxious all over again. She said, "Anna, you are going to inherit it and live here with us from now on. You don't have to go back. Look how happy you are here. We want you to stay."

That was a moment where I could have brought you up in the conversation, but I chose not to. I didn't want to risk losing my parents again. However, I also wasn't willing to give up on our love like I had done in the past. So, I let the moment pass without saying anything.

After three weeks, I finally managed to get in touch with Rekha. She is currently living with her family in Cochin. I made the decision to go and stay with her for a few days, and Ma and Pa were okay with it. I

opened up to   her about you and show   ed her
our pictures.

However, she then dropped a bombshell on
me. She revealed that Krishna, who is now
married and a father of two, is working at
a technology company very close to her
house. She asked if I wanted to see him.

I want to have an open conve   rsation with
you, John, about everyone in my life. I don't
want to keep anything hidden from you. I
fell deeply and quickly in love with you, and
it made me worry if it was just infatuation.
I also questioned my feelings for you   . A
delayed rebound   ? I asked   myself if I was
truly over him. I   believe   that taking some
time away from you would help me figure
things out as well.

During this time apart, I realized that I
missed you every day   , and my thoughts

were consumed by you. However, I thought that seeing Kr ishna again would be the ultimate test for me. I wanted to know how I truly felt or if I felt anything at all when I saw him.

So, on a Thursday, I went to Krishna's office. I went alone. When I arrived at the ground floor of his office building, I saw a si gn with his name on it. His office was located on the sixth floor, so I took the elevator up there. Once I reached his floor, I approached Krishna's office and asked to speak with him. His personal assistant came out to meet me, and I explained that I was an old friend and only needed 10 minutes of his time. I was then ushered into his office.

As I walked into his office, my mind was filled with thoughts. At any other time in my life, I would have been so happy to see him. However, I found myself entering with a neutral state of mind. It made me reflect on how life changes over time. How our feelings change, and how we change more precisely!!

As I stood at the door of Krishna's office, our eyes met, and he immediately broke into a warm smile. He hurried ove   r to me, pulling out a chair and gesturing for me to sit. "I can't believe it, Anna," he exclaimed, his voice filled with genuine surprise. I returned his smile and asked him how he was doing, curious about his well   - being.

 "Happy, " he said. As I looked a   t him, I couldn't help but notice the changes in his appearance. The youthful charm that once defined him had given way to a more mature and seasoned look. It was a stark reminder of the passage of time.

Taking a deep breath, I mustered the courage to express my apologies for disappearing from him years ago. To my relief, Krishna's smile remained intact as he reassured me that it was okay, that he had moved on. I couldn't help but feel a sense of relief and closure at that moment.

Wanting to share my happiness with him, I showed Krishna a picture of you. His eyes lit up as he remarked on your handsome features. However, despite his kind words, I couldn't help but notice that the spark and connection we once had were no longer present. The Krishna before me was different from the one I had known in the enchanting butterfly garden. It was a realization that struck me deeply.

At that moment, I came to understand that often, after a breakup and with the passage of time, what we hold onto and have a love

for is no   t truly the person themselves but
rather the memories we   share .

Back at home, Ma, Pa, and I established a
daily ritual. We would gather to have our
tea in the mornings.   Afterward   , Pa would
head to his shop, and sometimes   , I would
assist Ma with her tasks.   Other times, I
would grab a book and make my way down
to the nearby stream, where I would
immerse myself in its tranquil surroundings
and lose myself in the pages of my book.
The cool evening air embraced me as the
river continued to sing its timeless
melo dies, flowing gracefully around the
pebbles and rocks.

Nearly a month had passed since my
arrival, and I felt the need to briefly check
in with work to ensure there were no
pending tasks or responsibilities. I switched
on my computer and realized that ther   e

was another form I needed to fill out for my
FMLA. As I focused on completing the
necessary paperwork, Pa walked by and
inquired about what I was doing. I
explained that I was working on some
forms for my job.

"Are you certain that you're going back?" Pa
asked, his curiosity evident. Ma had joined
us in the room by now, sensing the weight
of the conversation. The moment had
arrived, and I knew I had to speak my truth.

Taking a deep breath, I mustered the
courage to share my decision. "I have to go,"
I began. "I am in a relationship with
someone named John. He treats me with
respect and love, Pa. Not once has he raised
his voice at me. I am happy with him. He
also has a   son. I want to go back to him.
The pictures Alex sent were meant to hurt
us, to seek revenge. But John is the only

man in my life, Pa, and I am not sleeping around with random men.   "

There was a brief silence in the room as Ma and Pa absorbed my words. Th   en, their expressions softened, and they both smiled. "When are you planning to go back?" Pa asked.

"I am going to start looking for tickets," I replied. "Early November seems like a good time, low prices before the holiday season.

I felt an overwhelming   sense of happiness. It felt like I had finally overcome the power that Alex held over me.

In the following weeks, Ma and I went on a pilgrimage to a church that she believed held miraculous powers. She asked me to make a pledge to attend five prayers fo   r marital happiness. Without hesitation, I agreed to fulfill her request. We visited

Parumala Church, where Ma handed me three candles to light in front of the altar. One was for me, one for you, and one for Noah.

One day, Pa asked me to join him in his Je   ep. He drove me to a local clothing shop and insisted that I choose silk Kurtas for you and Noah.

John, I can't pinpoint the exact moment when I realized you were the one for me during this journey. But I can tell you this. While walking with Rekha throug   h the narrow streets of Fort Kochi, a small beach town in Cochin with a lively Jewish culture and charming old shops, I would step into these small stores selling unique jewelry, antiques, handmade clothes, Kashmiri mats, and other old items. Whenever I en tered these stores, I would think to myself, "John would appreciate this or that."

I even asked the shopkeeper if he could send a big Kashmiri mat to another country. When Rekha asked why I wanted a mat, I said, " For our future home."

"Anna, it feels like you and John are already a married couple," she would say with a smile.

That's when I realized you had become a very important part of my life.

As time passed, I had this strong feeling that I wanted to come home and that home was with you.

Some days , whe n I didn't have anything important to do, I would explore the different rooms of the house. Each room held memories that were like invisible ink, written by the passing of time. Towards the back of the house, there is a narrow wooden staircase that leads t o the second floor. Up there, we have storage rooms where we keep dry spices. In one corner, there's a room with a big window and a wide windowsill. I used to sit there and write poems while watching the heavy rain during the monsoon season.

Recently, I w ent to that room and looked through some old books. Guess what I found? My old diary was there. It had a lot of poems written with a pencil ; although the writing has faded a bit, it's still readable. I kept it because I thought I could read it to you when I came home and share some happy memories from my childhood. That's how much I want to take you into my past and share it with you.

I haven't mentioned Naina much, but Ma told me she's doing well. A few days after I arrived, I was walking into the living room after taking a shower when I overheard Ma and Naina talking. I couldn't hear what Naina was saying, but I heard Ma say angrily, "Anna is not to blame. Yes, she went through a divorce, but that doesn't mean she's not our daughter. This is her home to o." When Ma saw me walking in, she quickly ended the phone call. After that, we didn't talk about it anymore.

Remember when I told you about the old mango tree I used to climb? Well, it's still standing there. I tried to climb it again, but I couldn't. How ever, I still had my old tricks. I used a long pole with a knot on top to pick the raw mangoes. I was sitting on the porch, enjoying them with salt and green chilies, when Ma came in with some whole spices. She started grinding them on the old stone grinder. She saw me eating the raw mangoes and said, "You still have these old habits. Now you have to change them, right? John wouldn't approve." I laughed and replied, "Ma, John has seen me eat raw mangoes before. He's seen me walk barefoot, let my wet hair dry naturally, and eat with my hands. I haven't changed for him, Ma. Sometimes, he's a little curious, but I can be myself with him more than anyone else. He doesn't expect me to be anyone else but me." I must say Ma has a great sense of humor. She jokingly said, "I'm sure John hasn't seen this old-fashioned stone grinder. You should take a picture of it for him." I agreed, and we laughed together for a long time.

My love, I know I wrote you a long letter, but I wanted to share everything with you.

Just two m   ore weeks, and I'll be by your
side. Once I have the flight details, I'll text
them to you, okay?

Forever yours,

Anna

Tears streamed down John's face as he read her words, his heart swelling with a mixture of relief, joy, and a profound sense of belonging. At that moment, he knew that their love was a force beyond reckoning, a bond that could withstand even the greatest of distances.

With renewed hope, John looked to the future with a sense of purpose. He knew that their paths would cross once more, that the universe would conspire to bring them back together. In the meantime, he would cherish every moment, every word, and every memory; he knew deep in his heart that he and Anna were bound by the invisible red string of destiny.

Their story was far from over; it was simply in a pause, waiting for the moment when they would once again step into the embrace of each other's arms.

After reading the letter a million times, John couldn't contain his excitement. He quickly texted Lilly and Jake.

Guess what? I heard from Anna! Everything is going well, and she'll be back in the first week of November."

Twenty-Nine

"The minute I heard my first love story, I started looking for you, not knowing how blind that was. Lovers don't finally meet somewhere. They're in each other all along."

— Rumi

Jake was busy planning his three-week annual leave, trying to reschedule his patients, find coverage, and cancel his upcoming appointments when Lilly walked into his office.

"Jake, I need to talk," Lilly stood there with unease and shadows of doubts creeping up her face.

Jake walked over to her with open arms, enveloping her in a warm embrace. "Oh, no, don't tell me that you cannot come with me, sister," he playfully teased, attempting to lighten the weight of her concerns.

A soft smile graced Lilly's lips as she reassured him, "I am coming with you, dear. That's not the issue."

Chuckling, Jake urged her to reveal the true nature of her thoughts. "Come on, confess now or forever hold your silence," he teased her.

"This is the issue, Jake. I mean, this marriage and everything that comes with it. You both made this life-altering decision in less than six months, and I cannot help but feel a twinge of worry. Don't you think it's too soon for such a huge commitment?"

Jake tried to explain, "Okay, I understand what you're saying. So, when you meet someone who could potentially be your partner, there's usually an initial attraction, like a spark or a strong physical connection. Then you go on dates and spend time getting to know each other. Both people start thinking about whether this person could be 'the one' for them. It's like a checklist of qualities and compatibility that you're looking for. Then there's the concept of arranged marriages, as Maya mentioned. In those cases, you're introduced to someone, and you also go through a process of checking if you like each other and have common goals and interests. But then there's our story: when I first met her, I felt something different. It wasn't just a physical attraction but more like an energetic pull. It felt like a deep spiritual connection between our souls. I couldn't ignore it or walk away from it. I don't know how to explain this connection because it doesn't fit into any specific category or explanation."

Lilly looked at Jake with a smile. "I'm sorry, dear, but I haven't personally experienced anything like what you're describing. I just wanted to make sure you were aware of what you were getting into. By the way, I need to go shopping for the wedding soon. I still haven't decided what to wear for your Hindu wedding, Jake."

"Lilly, I forgot to tell you that you don't have to go shopping for anything to wear for the wedding. Maya is getting both of our wedding outfits," Jake happily remembered.

"How does she know my size?" Lilly asked.

"I showed her a picture of you, so she will figure it out," Jake replied.

"Would you like to come with me to buy the ring?" Jake asked.

"Definitely!" Lilly replied.

Jake and Lilly went to a jewelry store after work.

Lilly asked Jake, "Are you going to get her the biggest diamond you can find?"

Jake laughed and replied, "No, Maya isn't into diamonds or rubies. That's not her style. I'm getting her an infinity ring instead. It symbolizes endless love, with no beginnings or ends."

Lilly responded, "That's beautiful."

Lilly was curious and asked, "You said it's going to be a Hindu wedding ceremony, right Jake?"

"Yes, I don't know much about it. Maya told me there would be a special ceremony called the 'varamala" or garland ceremony. They make a garland using flowers like jasmine and roses. The garland represents love, happiness, and beauty, all tied together with a string to symbolize the marriage. During the ceremony, the bride and groom exchange these garlands, which symbolize sharing spiritual energy with one another. By doing so, they become one spiritual being in two bodies".

"Very interesting," said Lilly.

"There's something even more special, Lilly. It's called the Saath pheras. First, the bride's wedding attire is tied to the groom's, symbolizing their love and connection. Then, they take seven rounds clockwise around a sacred fire, which acts as a witness to their spiritual union. The bride leads the first four rounds and is considered the main decision-maker in family matters and the household. The groom leads the remaining three rounds because he is seen as the provider and protector of the family. And the best part, Lilly, these seven rounds mean that we will be together not just in this life but for the next seven lives," Jake explained happily.

Lilly replied, "I'm excited about our upcoming trip, Jake. I've never seen anything like this before."

Jake put his arms around her as they waited for their cabs to arrive, feeling excited about the upcoming wedding ceremony.

Thirty

"This is love: to fly toward a secret sky, to cause a hundred veils to fall each moment. First to let go of life. Finally, to take a step without feet".

— Rumi

As November drew near, the final preparations for the wedding began to take shape. Jake booked their tickets, ensuring that he and Lilly would start their journey on the 7th of November and arrive at Cochin airport on the 8th. The anticipation grew, and Maya could hardly contain her excitement, knowing that Jake would soon be by her side, ready to embark on their new chapter together.

On the 5th of November, Jake excitedly sent a message to the Soul Haven group, sharing the news of his upcoming marriage to Maya.

I am getting married to Maya. Leaving on the 7th with Lilly, super happy, he wrote.

John, filled with joy for his friend, quickly replied, Congrats, Jake! Very happy for you. Anna will be back on the 7th as well. Maybe we can catch up at the airport."

Jake's heart swelled with gratitude as he responded, that would be awesome!

On the 7th, Jake, John, and Lilly eagerly waited at the airport, anticipating Anna's arrival before their departure. As Anna emerged, her face lit up with a radiant smile. She waved to Jake and Lilly, exchanging quick hugs before making her way over to John.

John's eyes sparkled with love and happiness as he embraced Anna tightly, showering her with kisses. Jake and Lilly, witnessing this beautiful moment, felt that this moment belonged to them and should not be disturbed. They quietly walked towards the departure gate.

And it was on the 7th that Maya and Siddh made the decision to drive to a nearby town and collect the wedding outfits.

Thirty-One

"Sorrow is knowledge; those that know the most must mourn the deepest; the tree of knowledge is not the tree of life."

— *Lord Byron*

Jake and Lilly got on the plane and got ready for the long journey ahead.

When the aircraft reached an altitude of 10,000 feet, Jake decided to unbuckle his seat belt and stand up. He was searching for the infinity ring he had bought for Maya.

"Lilly, I can't find the ring," Jake said, feeling disturbed.

"Are you sure you put it in your pocket?" Lilly asked.

"I took it off during the security check and placed it in my pocket," Jake replied.

Jake started to panic. "This feels like a bad sign," he kept repeating.

"Come on, Jake, it's just a ring. You can always get her a better one," Lilly tried to comfort him. "Try to get some sleep. It's going to be a long journey," Lilly reassured him.

Jake and Lilly arrived at Cochin airport in the early morning hours. Despite the oppressive heat and humidity, Jake's heart overflowed with joy at finally setting foot in India. As they made their way through the busy airport, Jake couldn't help but express his joy to Lilly. "Gosh, it's so hot and humid, but I am so grateful to be here."

Their eyes scanned the crowd, searching for Siddh, who patiently held a board with their names. Spotting him amidst the sea of faces, Jake and Lilly approached Siddh, enveloping him in a warm embrace. However, Lilly couldn't ignore the subtle shadows that seemed to cloud Siddh's expressions, hinting at a hidden sorrow.

Siddh informed them that their destination was a three-hour drive away. Sensing their exhaustion, he suggested that John and Lilly take a nap during the journey, assuring them that they would be awakened halfway for a refreshing tea break. The car journey commenced, the wheels turning as they ventured closer to their destination. Eventually, they reached the designated stop, where Sid asked Lilly to step out.

It was then that Siddh shared the heart-wrenching news. Lilly's anguished scream pierced the air, her soul shattered by the weight of the tragic revelation. Jake, sensing the magnitude of the situation, rushed out of the car, his heart pounding with a mixture of fear and disbelief.

Siddh tried to explain the best way he could, "Jake, while we were returning after picking up the wedding outfits, we got hit by a large truck at a bend in the road. The car spun uncontrollably, causing the driver to feel a complete loss of control. It careened around a bend and collided with a solid concrete barrier that separated the lanes. The impact was so forceful that the car flipped over before finally coming to a stop. Maya was trapped in the back; two men from the crowd swiftly grabbed a rod and shattered the window, allowing them to open the back door. We got Maya out and tried to revive her, but we couldn't! She died from a massive intracranial hemorrhage! I am so sorry, Jake; I wish it was me and not Maya." He sat on the ground and sobbed.

The details blurred together, leaving Jake disoriented and bewildered, only to awaken in a local hospital, his mind clouded by shock and grief.

The doctor gently explained the gravity of the situation to Jake. Recognizing the immense pain and emotional turmoil he was experiencing, he prescribed clonazepam to help him navigate through the overwhelming waves of sorrow. "You will need it," the doctor assured him, understanding the magnitude of his loss.

As Jake left the hospital, he felt the weight of his grief pressing upon him. The world around him seemed hazy, his heart heavy with sorrow. The road ahead appeared daunting, shrouded in darkness, and for the first time in his life, he felt devastated and defeated.

Thirty-Two

"I cannot let you burn me up, nor can I resist you. No mere human can stand in a fire and not be consumed."

— *Possession by A.S. Byatt*

Jake approached Maya's lifeless form, his heart heavy with grief. Sitting beside her, he gazed at her with unwavering eyes, refusing to blink except when tears blurred his vision. Each blink was a momentary respite from the overwhelming emotions that threatened to consume him.

From his pocket, he retrieved a small container of sindoor, a vivid red symbol of their sacred bond. With trembling hands, he delicately dipped his finger into the vibrant powder and traced it along the parting of Maya's hair. The red sindoor stood out against her pale skin, a poignant reminder of the love that once flourished between them.

Bending down, Jake pressed his lips gently against Maya's cold forehead, his breath mingling with the stillness of the room.

In a soft voice, he spoke the words that echoed his heart's deepest longing, "Forever mine."

In the tranquil embrace of the sacred Papanashini River, Jake embarked on a poignant journey accompanied by Maya's male cousins. As he immersed himself in the cool, crystalline waters, his tears merged with the gentle streams. Emerging from the river's tender caress, he was adorned in a white dhoti, a symbol of purity and reverence for the departed soul.

Back at Maya's house, the house, once a heaven filled with joy and laughter, was now filled with grief like a thick Fog. The flickering flame of a solitary lamp cast a soft, golden glow upon the room while the lingering scent of incense wafted through the air, intertwining with the echoes of sorrowful sobs. Guided by the wise Poojari, Jake was led to a secluded room where the ancient Hindu rites of cremation were explained.

The time had come to carry Maya to her final resting place by the river's edge. With utmost reverence and tenderness, the male members lifted the open casket, their hearts heavy with the weight of grief and the responsibility they bore. Jake followed in their footsteps. Behind him, Lilly stood alongside the female family members, their collective strength and unwavering support a silent pillar of solace.

As the families gathered, their voices hushed in reverence. Siddh was entrusted with a torch, its flickering flame a symbol of his role in this sacred ritual. The priest, a sage figure draped in wisdom, bestowed upon him the honor of igniting the pyre, a task that carried the weight of farewell and transformation.

Siddh approached the pyre with Jake by his side, its flames yearning for the touch of the torch. As he carefully brought the flame to the waiting wood, a spark ignited, and the fire began its mesmerizing dance, casting a warm, golden glow upon the surroundings. The crackling of the wood and the scent of burning filled the air.

In the presence of the sacred fire, Poojari's voice resonated, his prayers and rituals guiding Jake through this solemn moment. Amidst the flames that burned with a vengeance, Maya's physical form transformed, her essence transcending the earthly realm as if carried away by the flames into another dimension.

Time seemed to stand still as the fire gradually subsided, leaving behind a bed of ashes. The male members collected the remains.

That fateful night, as the weight of sorrow pressed upon Jake's soul, he found himself engulfed in the darkest depths of despair. The pain that gripped his heart was suffocating. It was as if his chest was being crushed under the weight of an indescribable anguish, threatening to consume him whole.

Seeking solace, he stumbled towards the window, desperate for a breath of fresh air to alleviate the torment that ravaged his spirit. The stillness of the night greeted him, its silence a haunting reminder of the emptiness that now permeated his existence. He longed to sleep, hoping to find temporary respite from the relentless ache that plagued him. Instead, he felt himself being pulled deeper into an abyss of darkness, a never-ending tunnel devoid of any flicker of light.

In the midst of his despair, Jake struggled to comprehend the inexplicable nature of his love for Maya, a love that transcended continents and defied all logic. From the moment their eyes met, he had known with unwavering certainty that she was his soulmate, destined to be his forever. The memories of their connection, even in past life regression sessions, echoed in his mind. But now they seemed distant and incomprehensible, slipping through his fingers like grains of sand. One memory, however, stood out amidst the chaos. He remembered pleading with Tom to conduct a progressive life session in the future, but Tom had refused, claiming that Maya did not want it.

At that moment, a realization washed over Jake. She knew. She knew that their time together was limited and that she would soon depart from this world. It was as if she possessed a glimpse into the future. In the depths of his despair, Jake reached a devastating conclusion - it was the end. There seemed to be no way forward, no glimmer of light to guide him out of the suffocating darkness. As he approached the table by the window, his eyes fixated on the bottle of clonazepam, a small vessel of temporary relief from the torment that plagued his mind. The allure of escape beckoned him, his hand trembling as it reached out to grasp the bottle, ready to surrender to the consuming darkness that enveloped him.

But just as he was about to succumb to the seductive call of oblivion, a sudden gust of wind tore through the stillness of the night, shattering the suffocating silence. The force of the wind knocked over the glasses on the table, sending them crashing to the floor and scattering the medicines in a chaotic dance. The sound of the commotion jolted Jake from his despair, startling him out of the depths of his anguish. It was as if the universe itself had intervened, refusing to let him surrender to the abyss.

Lilly's heart raced with alarm as she entered the room, her eyes widening at the sight of a disoriented and broken Jake surrounded by the scattered remnants of his despair. Without hesitation, she rushed to his side, her voice filled with concern and urgency. "Oh no, Jake, what were you thinking?" she exclaimed, her voice trembling with worry.

Jake, overwhelmed by his own anguish, found comfort in Lilly's presence. He clung to her tightly, his body trembling with the weight of his sorrow. "I didn't know how to go on, Lilly," he whimpered, his voice choked with tears.

Lilly held him close, her arms a comforting shield against the storm that raged within him. She allowed him to release his sorrow, his wails echoing through the room as he let his heartache dissolve into tears. She remained steadfast, a pillar of strength, offering unwavering support as he navigated the depths of his despair.

When Jake's cries subsided, Lilly spoke with a voice filled with love and determination. "I have lost so many in my life, Jake. I don't want to lose my brother. Promise me," she pleaded, her eyes searching his, "promise me that you will never think of this ever again."

Lilly gently guided Jake to the bed, sitting beside him, her touch a soothing balm for his wounded soul. She ran her fingers through his hair. "You are my brother," she whispered, her voice filled with love. "And I will be with you every step of the way. I don't want you to ever give up, Jake. And know in your heart, Maya will always be with you."

Lilly sat by Jake's bedside until his weary eyes succumbed to the embrace of sleep. With a gentle touch, she brushed a stray lock of hair from his forehead. As the moon cast its soft glow upon the room, she quietly began to pack their bags, knowing that their journey awaited them the following evening.

Thirty-Three

"He stepped down, trying not to look long at her, as if she were the sun, yet he saw her, like the sun, even without looking."

— Anna Karenina by Leo Tolstoy

The next day arrived, and Jake carried himself with a stoic demeanor. The priest returned to complete the remaining rituals. The day unfolded with the Pooja, a sacred ceremony that spanned hours. Jake and Lilly sat beside Maya's grieving parents, finding comfort and peace in their shared presence. Amidst the chanting and prayers, Jake felt a strange sense of consolation, as if Maya's spirit was guiding him through the rituals, offering a glimmer of peace amidst the sorrow. When the Pooja was over, Jake spoke for the first time since he arrived.

"Amma and Achen, I came here to take my girl home with me. Can I take her with me, I mean the ashes?"

The family was silent, and they looked at each other but did not utter a word.

As the time to depart for the airport approached, Jake embraced Amma. "I will be back," he said. "Where is Achen?" he asked, his eyes searching for him.

Achen then walked from the bedroom with Siddh carrying an Urn. He placed the Urn in Jake's hands and said, "This is not how I wanted to give her away in marriage to you, but this is all I have now. She belongs with you. Take her with you."

Jake folded his hands and said, "Thank you, Achan and Amma." He placed the Urn in his bag and walked to the car with Lilly.

Lilly and Jake entered the car in silence, their thoughts and emotions swirling within them. The journey to Cochin airport was marked by a profound silence as if the weight of their grief had rendered them speechless.

As the plane's engines hummed to life and the aircraft accelerated down the runway, Jake's gaze shifted to the illuminated city of Cochin below, a jewel nestled by the Arabian Sea. He turned to Lilly, his voice mixed with sadness and love, and said, "I am taking my girl with me."

Lilly smiled gently. "She is with you. You will start to feel her presence more and more beyond the confines of this dimension.

She is a part of you, forever intertwined in your heart and soul now."

As the plane soared higher into the vast expanse of the sky, Cochin faded away, and the world below became a mere speck in the grand tapestry of existence. In that vastness, closer to the heavens, Jake felt a stirring within his being.

As the aircraft gracefully maneuvered its final turn, gliding over the vast expanse of the Arabian Sea, he reached into his bag, his fingers searching for the familiar touch of the blue shawl that Maya used to playfully drape around herself, teasing him endlessly. As he pulled it out, a rush of memories flooded his mind, each thread of the fabric holding a piece of their shared love.

With a tender touch, he wrapped the shawl around his neck, feeling the softness against his skin. It was as if Maya's presence enveloped him, her essence lingering in the delicate fibers. The scent of her, a unique blend of warmth and love, filled his senses, transporting him to a place where distance and time held no power.

With a mix of love, longing, and grief, Jake powered on his phone, his heart pounding in his chest. As the screen illuminated, his eyes were drawn to Maya's final message.

"To my eternal love, I love you to the end of the universe and back, and I promise to be with you for all eternity. Never doubt it."

www.ingramcontent.com/pod-product-compliance
Lightning Source LLC
Chambersburg PA
CBHW071555150726
48000CB00004B/1467